Clouds, Dreams & Fantasy

Also by Linda L. Flynn:

Women's Lit:

Dream Glasses
Finding the Way Home

Family Stories:

Flynn Tales
Stories by Elizabeth (Bess) Flynn & James (Jimmy) Flynn

Granny's Legacy
Recipes from the collection of
Dorothy Helen (Hall) Stauffacher

Children's Stories:

Gabriel and the Bear
The Big Adventure

Clouds, Dreams & Fantasy

Linda L. Flynn

jouneytotheheights.com

Copyright © 2023 AppleWood Press

ISBN-13: 978-1-7321864-4-6

Dreams, Clouds & Fantasy is dedicated to those who survived Covid-19 and the changes wrought by the Pandemic. Life for all of us was upended. We each have our own stories of this experience. Perhaps this book will help you find your voice of survival or endurance for this time. It is my hope you will feel connection or find pleasure in these writings.

Table of Contents

Acknowledgements and Backstory

The writings for *Clouds, Dreams & Fantasy* took shape during the Pandemic and cover the timeframe of 2020-2022. I lived in a state where the Governor locked down social gatherings.

Having just arrived home from an extended stay in Ireland, my writer friends there asked if I would be interested in joining them for Zoom writing meetings. We were able to coordinate an agreeable time. Those meetings continue.

The Carbondale Writers Group, (Carbondale, CO), transitioned from monthly, in person meetings to weekly Zoom meetings.

Lisa Jones, a writer, teacher and storyteller, sent an email to friends who'd previously taken one of her classes to solicit interest in joining a FaceBook writing group for several weeks. She had some down time, as the University cancelled classes while trying to establish their plan for Covid. Through this group, I connected with more writers.

I don't remember how I connected with Kerstin Pilz, PhD, but I did. She was in Vietnam, and has an on-line site WriteYourJourney. I subscribed to her newsletters, which contain a writing prompt or two. Now and again, I would come across someone else's writing prompts.

I owe heart-felt thanks to each of these groups, they provided inspiration and focus.

These writing communities, often unlocked potential and stories I didn't know were within me. Friendships deepened, or developed. Creatives bonded and encouraged one another. No matter our geographical locations we were all impacted by Covid-19.

I'm indebted to my husband who kept encouraging me to pull away and write. He witnessed the value of investing in creativity during those uncertain days.

I refer to this as my Pandemic writing, only because of the time frame from which most of these writings were created. Little of it is about Covid-19, but that is what you'll discover when you read the book.

Lastly, thank you to my readers. From all the titles out there that you could pick from, thank you for choosing my book. I hope you enjoy it!!

Linda xx

Linda

Listless thoughts
Indulge the mind
Nothing accomplished
Drifting clouds
Await slumber

The Cat Set Me Free

Lessons Learned from Living with a Cat

Watching the animal soaking in the sun while stretching on the carpet,

I realized how I longed for the confidence to simply be comfortable and unpretentious anywhere.

Oh! She saw me then came to perch on the arm of the chair and sit beside me.

She exhibited such elegance yet maintained a sense of ownership.

She knew what was hers and was not threatened by my presence or anyone else.

Lazily, she lay down on the chair arm, tucking her front paws under her.

Her purring reminded me to find contentment in all situations.

Occasionally I would reach over to touch her soft fur and ponder how finely she was clothed.

All afternoon she sat with me

Reminding me of patience and acceptance.

She sat up, stretched, put her face close to mine for a moment

Then scampered off to another room in the house.

Reminding me

No one can be owned.

Hotel Paradise

Stretched out on an oversized chaise lounge, I gazed around the room. I couldn't believe I was in a tropical paradise. We'd picked this resort because of its proximity to the sea and to the amenities afforded tourists in the trendy shops and restaurants. Sailboats were available for rental on the bay. We would spend at least one day on the turquoise sea, allowing the ocean wind to propel the boat through the water. Just the thought of the large sail causing the boat to keel peaked my sense of adventure and thrilled my heart.

My attention was more immediately directed to the room where I sat. Tom had dropped our bags, kissed me on the head, and promised to return with treats after he'd arranged for the boat rental. I kicked off my shoes, grabbed my latest read and settled into this chair. Heavy canvas curtains tied back revealed a wide view of the shore, creating a sense of the beach being just beyond the window. I knew we would close these curtains later to shut out the surrounding world. Pillows of various shapes and sizes covered an oversized canopy bed against one wall, inviting one to snuggle in and get comfortable. I imaged us later enjoying our morning coffee at the small café table and chairs in-front of the windows. But for now, I stretched out on the chaise and wiggled my toes. I longed to have some quiet time to read. I found myself engrossed in this intensely suspenseful story and eager to return to the plot. Tom being gone for a while presented the window for escape I needed. I reopened the pages and expected to be instantly caught up in the story, but I couldn't focus on the words. A gentle breeze blew through the room. The fragrant salty air took my mind to thoughts of sailing into the sunset. The wind rustled through the trees. Street vendors traversed the streets, calling out to passersby. They were so noisy; they interrupted my thoughts. I failed to understand why others had to be so loud and did not savor the tranquil atmosphere provided by the sun, waves, and fresh air. As I glanced around the room, the atmosphere calmed me and other thoughts filled my mind.

"Why am I here?"

Tom wanted to sail again, I wanted to relax, and we both wanted a romantic break from our hectic schedules. Somehow, the sun bleached room appeared inviting and serene, not old and worn. Housekeeping strategically placed several tropical floral arrangements around the room awaiting our arrival. I was sure we had made an excellent choice when we picked this resort.

I felt relaxed and peaceful as I returned to my book. Out of the corner of my eye, I thought I saw something move beneath the carpet. And then not. No! My eyes must be playing tricks on me. I went back to my read. Distracted again, I looked around. Nothing. Another disturbance. I furtively gazed around the room. It happened again! A hump moved through or below the carpet. It appeared about the size of a melon in diameter. First, I saw it slide beneath the carpet for a foot or two, then it disappeared. What was happening? What could this be? And what did it mean? Though the breeze continued to blow through the windows and cause the trees outside to sway, it was no longer calming. My heart pounded. I wanted Tom to return and tell me everything would be 'just fine.' Though my book was on my lap, it held no interest. I continued peering around the room, expectant of what might happen next.

After what seemed like forever, Tom returned. He took one look at me, dropped the white box on the table top, then rushed to the chaise. Asking what was wrong, I attempted to tell him what I had seen. He laughed that laugh which always warms my heart and makes me happy and secure, then said, "You have such a vivid imagination. You should write children's stories."

I laughed with him, but wasn't relieved. The fragrance of fresh bakery goods wafted throughout the room and tempted me to rush over to the table to learn what treats we had. There nestled in the bakery tissue laid fine flaky pastries, some with icing and some with sugar and cinnamon toppings. They looked and smelled delicious. We elected to save them for later and settled back into the chaise lounges to talk about the sights he'd seen and make plans for the rest of the trip.

Lost in conversation and excited about how we would enjoy the island, I relaxed. We both heard it! A loud tearing sound as the carpet ripped, and this THING broke through, revealing a body about eight inches in width. This THING was shaped like a snake with short mottled black and brown fur; its snake shaped head displayed features of a dog with flaming eyes. It looked at me and snarled. Then bared its teeth. I screamed!

Men in uniforms marched the streets with megaphones and called out, "Attention! Attention! If you have sweets in your room, you must move them to your refrigerator. I repeat, you must store all your food in the refrigerator. These creatures you see want your food, especially anything sweet. They will remain as long as they detect any food." They kept repeating this message first in English, followed by other languages as they walked the streets.

I froze on the chaise lounge. I desperately wanted my shoes and to be gone from here, but instead found myself frozen. Tom jumped up and started rushing around, gathering up the treats and shoving them into the refrigerator. My last memory was Tom picking up my shoes, holding out his hand as he said, "Come on! We need to get out of here!"

I turned to run, but instead rolled over, opened my eyes and realized I lay safe in my own bed. My heart pounded and my breathing was fast and shallow, but I smiled as I thought, *Sometimes paradise is closer than you imagine.*

The Voice of God

The voice of God is small, fond, and local.

It is that small tranquil voice calling to you in the still of night, or whispering to you amidst the din surrounding you. You can pretend it isn't there, or that he doesn't speak to you. Then something happens and he'll be speaking to some place deep within you.

After learning to listen for this voice, I find comfort in how familiar his voice can be. That doesn't mean I always like or appreciate what he says to me. It's the fact that he's there, fully aware of what's going on within me, around me and to me. There's comfort in such familiarity; security in knowing he's there for the long haul—longer than I can comprehend.

This comfort and security are my rock during these times. I'm absolved from the culpability of knowing or even explaining what's happening or why. I know I'm asked to be diligent and wise, to act responsibly even though I don't know the outcome.

My days now consist of trying to be responsible through things I don't understand; working to stay in contact with family and friends scattered far and wide; trying to cement the importance of relationship in a different way; seeking to be relevant to others, all while remaining within my home.

Cousins

Five we were.
Three girls, two boys bonded by blood.
Twin mothers.

Closer to them than my sibling.
The boys and I the older group
my sis and theirs the younger.
Hours upon hours we spent together.

Those simple days morphed into years.
From children to adults we became.
Each traversing our own path.
Time would make it seem
our connections lost
until some event would again reunite us.
New alliances developed.

The familiarity among this group
provides comfort.
Shared history sheds insight
into who each of us are.
Though bonded by blood
we recognize the uniqueness of each.

Perplexing to accept
we've become the aged
of our family tree.

The Sea

life's journey

The sound of the sea
  in a small voice
  beckoned to me.

I heeded not the call
  and became known
  as wife and mother to all.

To the heartland I returned
  where I gave my children wings
  and the title 'wife' was burned.

Many years passed
  and in the same heartland I found
  the love of my life at last.

And by the sea
  we exchanged our vows with no thought
  of the call which once beckoned me.

Going Home

...means different things to different people

Shirley awoke early. She tried to keep her breathing even and quiet, tried to hide the excitement welling within her. She didn't want to wake Bill. This was 'her day'. She'd planned it for weeks. The night before, she emptied her work locker of everything except the bare essentials. Her briefcase, packed and ready, waited by the door. The cookies she baked last night for her dad waited on the counter. Everyone expected her to visit her dad before leaving on a business trip where she would be away from home and her family for three weeks. What no one realized, she planned a second interview for a position in her hometown. Weary of the traveling required to visit family, she looked for a job closer to home. There were friends in her hometown. She tossed and turned. After all the years she chased Bill from town to town for his job, she felt it was time for her to decide where they lived. She realized her kids would not want to move. They liked their school. They had friends here, but she reasoned Jake was a freshman. He could make new friends. Ted was in seventh grade. Would it really matter? She knew Bill would be resistant, as he yearned for community and church involvement. Because they called her back for another interview, she expected they would offer her the job. She understood she should tell Bill. But he wouldn't understand and she wasn't ready for the discussion to follow. He didn't get it! She didn't want to exert the effort in another community again. She wanted to go home. Home, where she recognized the people who ran the local grocery and hardware stores. Home, to recall the memories of days past and walk on the familiar streets again.

Without realizing it, she drifted back to sleep. "Darn!" The alarm clock jarred her awake. Shirley turned it off, slipped out of bed and tip-toed to the bathroom where she showered, applied her makeup, curled her hair and dressed. Taking a second look in the mirror, she thought, Yes, everything about me looks good today!

She walked to the bed, bent, and gently shook Bill's shoulder.

She leaned over, kissed his cheek, and quietly said, "Sorry to wake you, but I wanted to say goodbye before I left."

In a groggy voice, he said, "Be safe and remember, I love you."

"I love you too. I'll make sure the kids get off to school before I leave. See you tonight."

She entered the kitchen with her mind wandering. Will I ever be able to sleep as late as I please? Retirement must be nice.

Both of the kids finished their breakfast and grabbed their backpacks.

"Hey, don't I get a kiss before you leave?"

They hugged and kissed their mom, turned and ran out the door.

Jake yelled back, "See you tonight. Love you."

Shirley smiled and thought, I have two great sons!

She grabbed her briefcase and the cookies for her dad as she headed out the door. It was a beautiful morning. The sun was peeking out from the wispy clouds hovering close to the horizon. The drive to Peshtigo would be peaceful. As soon as she got in the car, she turned on the music. She was glad to be traveling back to her hometown and sang along with some tunes on the radio as she watched the countryside slip past her. She played through the potential interview questions. Shirley was confident about this job. Her qualifications and references were stellar. She had to figure out how she would return tonight, tell Bill and the kids we're moving again. Could she convince them it really was the proper job for her, the ideal town, and the perfect move for them? They would have to understand!

Before she realized it, she pulled into the driveway of her old home. Shirley hopped out of the car, grabbed the cookies, and started up the front steps. The familiar creak at the top of the steps caused her to smile. Dad sat at the kitchen table, reading the paper and enjoying a cup of coffee.

"Why Shirley, you're here earlier than I expected," he said.

She watched him try to rise; and she rushed to the cupboard.

"Dad, don't get up. I remember where everything is and I'll get myself a cup of coffee. Then we can talk."

As they sat drinking their coffee, he filled her in on the happenings of the town. They talked about the flowers mom would miss this year.

Shirley said, "We should take a bouquet to the cemetery after we eat lunch."

He looked pleased with this idea. They went to the garden and cut an enormous bunch of daises, phlox, delphinium, and even found a hydrangea in full bloom. After putting them in a large pail of water, they drove to Brenda's Cafe for sandwiches. Shirley enjoyed a sense of safety caused by being in a familiar locale where change wasn't constant. They finished lunch and drove to the cemetery, where they placed the flowers at the gravesite. They remember the woman buried there. Shirley glanced at her watch and realized she had to take her dad home and get to the interview. As they drove home, her dad complained about her upcoming business trip. He wasn't happy she'd be far from family for so long. Shirley just laughed this off.

"Dad, it won't be that long and I'll be back home. You won't even realize I'm gone."

Thirty minutes later, Shirley sat in the lobby, confident and ready for the interview.

"Mr. Smith is prepared to see you now," said the receptionist. She stood and was ushered into the conference room.

The focal point of the office was a large round table centered in-front of a wall of windows. The view overlooked the river. Caught up in the view, Shirley almost forgot she was there for an interview.

"Would you care for a glass of water, coffee or soda before I leave?" asked the receptionist.

"No thank you."

Shirley turned her thoughts back to the interview.

Mr. Smith entered the room and said, "Hi Shirley. I hope you had a pleasant drive this morning."

"Yes. It was a lovely drive. I even had time to visit with my dad before our appointment."

"I'm sure you reviewed the job position we sent. We are very interested in the skills you bring to the position we have."

This was going as Shirley hoped. The next hour and a half flew by as he offered her the position and they worked out the details of her employment contract. Shirley's heart beat with anticipation!

Mr. Smith said, "The only outstanding things are signing the agreement and the drug screening tests. If you want to do the drug screening today, our lab is open. I could have the paperwork ready for you to sign in about 30 minutes.

Then you wouldn't need to make a special trip and we'd have everything done."

"Yes, that would be great! I'd like to have the details all taken care of."

Mr. Smith gave her directions to the lab and told her they would be ready for her when she arrived.

Before she knew it, she finished at the lab and returned to the lobby. The receptionist directed her into the conference room where Mr. Smith was waiting with the papers on the table. She sat down.

"Thank you for suggesting we take care of the details today. Now when I go home, I can share with my family the exciting news of this job. We'll be able to plan for the move."

They both stood, and Mr. Smith shook Shirley's hand.

"We're eager for you to join our company and will see you in about six weeks. Again, thank you for your time."

Shirley stepped into the lobby, glanced around again and knew she'd be content here!

Before leaving town, Shirley wanted to spend a few minutes savoring the atmosphere of the place she called 'home'. At the local Dairy Queen, she ordered a Peanut Buster Parfait, found an empty booth where she settled in to watch people and savor the thought of living here while she enjoyed her ice cream. She wondered, could this be real? Can I come home? As these thoughts raced through her mind, she lost track of time. Suddenly, she realized it was late. She needed to return to Bill and the kids. With carefree thoughts and happy dreams, she left Dairy Queen and got into her car to head back to her family.

The sun was setting, and the thrill of the day waning, she couldn't help but ponder why her father was so anxious over her upcoming trip. It was so unlike him to behave this way. Her thoughts drifted to how Bill would react when he found out she had gone on an interview, accepted a job, and planned to move the family again. Oh, how would the kids react when she set things in motion and they'd have to say goodbye to their friends? She thought, maybe it's good I'm leaving for this business trip. Perhaps everyone will be over the surprise when I return. She didn't realize how much these thoughts had distracted her driving until she heard a horn blare. She glanced up and saw the big red semi heading straight toward her, but she had no time to react. Her thoughts drifted to her boys—oh, her boys! She squeezed her eyes shut and gripped the steering wheel. She heard screeching rubber on the road as the truck driver slammed on his brakes. The truck hit the front of the car with a grinding squeal. The deafening sound of metal crunching and twisting filled the air as the car started folding together like an accordion; loud shattering noise and glass flew everywhere when the windshield exploded; as the truck scraped the entire driver's side of the car, twisted and torn metal sprayed out from the vehicle. The truck came to a sudden stop and everything went black for Shirley.

Bill finished cleaning up dinner; the boys were in the family room watching TV when the doorbell rang.

"I'll get it," said Bill.

When Bill opened the door, he saw Sheriff Adams standing there.

"Why, Richard…"

Sheriff Adams touched Bill's arm.

"Bill, I'm sorry. When I received the report, I promised to come. You're my friend."

"What's happened? Is Shirley okay?"

Richard looked down and shook his head.

"I'll need you to come with me. I'll drive, then bring you home later. That way, we can talk. Let the boys know you are leaving with me."

"Ok. I'll tell the boys, get my jacket and be right back."

When Bill returned, Richard put his arm around Bill's shoulder and they headed to the squad car.

The next hours were a blur. Bill couldn't remember the phone calls he made, the people he talked to, or the papers he signed. It was dark when Richard brought him back to the house. Richard hugged him and said he'd check on him in the morning.

When Bill entered the family room, the boys knew something was wrong. He asked the boys to sit next to him on the couch and he told them their mother had died in a car / truck collision earlier in the evening. They sat together, hugging and crying until late. When each trudged off to their own room, their shoulders were slumped, heads hung low, while they methodically placed one foot in front of the other.

Bill fell into his bed, still not able to comprehend Shirley wouldn't be crawling into bed later that night, or ever. Why did she have to visit her father today, and not be at work? Why hadn't they talked more about the day's plans? He couldn't fathom answers to these questions tonight and he didn't understand how this change would become 'his reality'. No matter what the changes would be for him and the kids, he recognized Shirley got her wish—she had gone home!

Wind Rider

Riding the breeze

A perfect day it was
Sky blue
Breeze light
To be a MacGregor day date

Sailing novice
I am not
I can do what I'm told
yet understand not
how to play the wind
My husband calls me
his 'First Mate'

Full sails skimming across the lake
I notice waves turning to white caps
little realizing I could be bait

To the mooring we returned
with little choice
but to sail into the wind
Novice I am
I pondered our fate

But tying off was not to be for me
Lost my balance and overboard I went
leaving my husband in quite a strait

Neighbors to the rescue
With laughter and much work
the boat was again tied to the crate

For the elements
new respect I have gained
We laugh of the event
still looking for blue skies and wind
we do wait

Mermaid Child

I thought I gave birth to a baby girl. We were to live as a family on the land. I presumed she was mine. I soon learned this was not true. From a young age, this child displayed a rebellious and defiant spirit as out of control as the ocean during a tumultuous storm, against everything that had the scent of tradition, authority, or rules. Occasionally, I would have fleeting glimpses of the daughter I thought was mine. And then they would be gone! Hers became a dance of seeing how far she could stray from the line. The collateral damage and destruction of those she either hurt or destroyed in her dance of defiance was huge. Every time I looked, the circle became larger. It included individuals both close to her, and those just touched by the fringes of her life, and people whom she once charmed and since grew tired of. Then a while back we vacationed with her at the beach. Those few short days were a gift. Time spent together was pleasant and devoid of the stress I associated with her. I realized something about the ocean seems to calm the rage she has toward life and civilization. She moved back inland again, and the glimpses I saw of her at the ocean vanished. Is the ocean her true home and not this land the rest of us live on? Perhaps she was not a baby girl, but a baby mermaid instead. Perhaps she was never mine at all.

A conversation with my local pastor triggered these thoughts when he challenged me to consider an age when she was innocent before all the problems began (which brought to mind a photo of her sitting on the beach when she was about three, wearing a white swimming-suit with red and blue polka dots) and then a conversation with my husband pointed out how the vacation trip we took with this child was such a gift. We spent almost a full week together, and it was a week of no stress, no drama, no troublesome times, just pleasant time together. I'm glad I could frame this vacation into the image of a 'normal gift' with this child because my life history with her did not allow me many of those memories. Somehow those two images merged into the Mermaid Girl—I decided those words may describe her!

She has since returned to ocean-side living, where she's more in control of her life and emotions. For me, these changes create a situation where I find it pleasant to spend time with her. I still can't answer if she's a mermaid or a woman, but she's beautiful.

The Grass is Greener

(Parting words in 2020 to the Tralee Writers)

As much as I've enjoyed traipsing around to take advantage of beautiful sites, I've discovered the biggest blessing is getting to know people in different locations. I've learned we may have a different life story, may look different, and may choose differently in any situation. Yet, most often, I've noticed at the core, all people want similar things. We want to be accepted and respected; we want to feel we bring something of value to life; we want to feel safe; we want assurance we won't go hungry and we don't want to be judged negatively for our beliefs.

Simple as it sounds, differences in life values can create challenges to living this out.

The grass actually is greener in Ireland than in Colorado.

The sky is bluer in Colorado than Ireland.

Both conditions provide natural beauty, albeit unique beauty.

I've found during my time in Ireland that I enjoy the natural beauty; however, it's the culture and the people who have captivated my heart. When I think of this group, I have affectionate feelings. Thank you for making me feel so welcome, allowing me to feel at home with you and allowing me to share my writings and for your support and encouragement. This is a safe environment for me.

The Virus

April 2020

When released to be free after centuries of being locked within only one species, I finally had the opportunity for my greatest prize. I jumped from animal to human, unsure of what would happen to me. Would I live in a different host? Would I thrive or die? I made the leap, and things begin to happen. I discovered I could live in a man. Man's movements and social interactions would bring me into contact with more men than I imagined. Oh, and how easy it was to jump from one human to another. At first, I made these movements undetected. Even the man was unaware of my existence, yet that didn't feed my growing feelings of independence and importance. I found if I remained silent within the man, I could multiply within him and others. Then, after I had grown within humans, I made myself known. I learned a lot about man during the weeks when I was just growing strong and multiplying within him. I studied the man and learned he likes control, control of his life and circumstances around him. Soon I revealed myself. I attacked his body. I made him ache; I made him cough until his breathing became difficult. Eventually, he sought help from others of his kind who thought they had the power to heal. Some of these healers helped, but many of them were unaware I had already invaded their precious bodies as well. I continued to grow, to gain power, and to mutate. I was unaware of how unmeasurable man's mobility was and how vast my control would become. Yes. I was in control, invading human bodies worldwide. Ok, so some recovered, but many died. It was because of me, because of the power I wielded.

Now I look at man, racing time in an effort to control my growth; trying to limit my reach for power and growth. Oh, did I say power? Yes, I can understand how a man comes to desire power. When you get attention, it feeds something within and you want more. So, yes, I want more power. I want greater recognition of how impactful I am. See, over there—entire cities have shut down. I have overtaken the world. Who has the power now? Oh, latest news flash—countries have closed their borders. Man's movement is limited; no longer can he roam the earth at will.

I heard some scientists are studying me. What do they hope to find? How to become as powerful as me? Suggestions include they are looking for an immunization to neutralize me. Really? They think they can do that. Well, we'll see...

What Isolation is Like for Me

My mind immediately thinks surreal. After moving to the mountains in 2012, I've fantasized about an occasion when I might be sequestered in my home. My fantasy was connected to a big snowstorm. Yet now I'm in my home, because of an invisible, fast moving, indiscriminate virus advancing through the population.

First, thoughts of needing to stay home generated an enormous sigh. Finally, I can stay home and catch up on things I've been longing to do; or things I've left undone while focusing on travel and other activities.

My husband and I both like to cook, and we both love the area where we live, and we enjoy spending time together. Add to those positives, we've an apartment remodel project in the works. All is well at our house.

For me, the problems surfaced when I realized I couldn't muster the energy to do some tasks left undone around here. I approached my messy office with a feeling of dread at having to sort through things I'd left stack up in there during the last year when I was traveling. Ugh! The house is quiet, unless we have music on. Tom retreated to the lower level to continue the cabinetry install and start laying the flooring. I worked through stacks of papers, mail and travel information, sorting things into recycle, file and yet another "wait for another day" pile. After a week, the double walled desk area is ready and waiting for me to return to either art or writing in the room. (The sewing cabinet still needs attention–but not today.)

Several mornings we have awoken to fresh snow. The beauty of the white reminds me of how God makes things clean, even me. I love how the spring snow with its high moisture content piles up on the tree branches and left over tall grasses from last year. On those very special days, the blue sky against the white creates such a vibrant contrast. On these spring days, when the sun is shining, the beautiful contrast created by the snow vanishes before lunch. Yet it creates such a tranquil splendor and starts my day in an upbeat swing. I step on the deck and the sounds of the birds fill the air. Our neighborhood is quiet, so this experience is consistent with other days. Sounds have changed little. Most days, we can count the cars that drive on our loop. These days there are even fewer. I like the quiet. The quietness and the view make living here peaceful. Bonus: Because the newest neighbors are working from home, they've experienced just how incessantly their dogs bark and have brought them into the house more. Perhaps there will be improvement when the freedom to move comes again.

Meals have been more of a treat, at least the dinner meals. Being home affords more time to plan and prepare, so we've been trying some different recipes and savoring the flavors. That results in the kitchen smells overflowing into the house; fragrances of different spices and combinations of vegetables; and grilled meat. Yum! I'm glad we indulge in this daily treat. The flavors have been great! Is it due to spending more time in meal preparation, and the meals feel less hurried, or is there some bigger message being communicated? I don't know, but it brings us together to sit at the table, enjoy the flavors and our conversation.

We are probably reading too much news these days; me more than Tom. Both of us look for inputs nationally and internationally. We discuss the news and the contacts we've each had throughout the day. We're spending so much more time on the computer or phones–keeping up with friends and family across the US, local friends, and friends in Ireland, England and Germany. I've had more interactions with adult grandchildren as we've talked about changing plans and they confirm that grandpa and I are taking care of ourselves. Their concern is sweet. But sweeter still are the developing relationships happening because we are all functioning slower. With fewer distractions and the reduction of some clutter removed from our lives, we have more time to reflect on the individuals who enrich our lives, those we love and care about. This is a positive thing for me.

Being home has allowed greater time to spend on the property. The tuffs of green grass are springing up in various places. The deer have returned from the lower elevations and are eagerly nibbling on these tiny tuffs. They seem so glad to have returned. They are almost oblivious to us when we're outside as well. My daffodils are poking through the ground with their strong, erect, dark green leaves. Within the leaves are signs of buds forming. One day soon, their yellow cheerful faces will display and declare "Spring has Come", then I will smile, as I always do because daffodils are happy flowers. The blue birds have returned as well. And the yellow finch, they are gaining their summer finery. Tom has been busy pruning and getting the civilized part of the yard back under control.

The morning air smells of fresh sage brought to life from the moisture of the snow.

I expect this time of separation to change each of us. For me, it may be a continuation of the changes begun in me after traveling out of the country for ten weeks.

Code Readers

Writing births writing. And so it was with this piece.
As part of a group, we heard several poems by Alison Luterman. Then we were turned lose to write.
Words spur inspiration.

Coded ways I say "I love you" and other things

It's morning – a peaceful sunny morning at our house.

I sneak out of the bedroom as quietly as I can to allow my hubby additional zz's.

Snuggling downstairs, I pick up a book to read – but only after getting absorbed in some of the latest news. Gads! I wish I wasn't such a news junkie these days.

He quietly comes downstairs and opens the blinds to let the morning light into the house.

The light, so welcome after a good night's sleep.

I get up to make his French Press coffee.

A simple routine, but one done as a demonstration of love.

I don't drink coffee, yet for me, it's important to do this for him.

"I love you."

We FaceTime with friends from southern England.

Afternoon here, evening there.

They look so amazingly healthy and peaceful.

We each chat about the things we're doing now that we're out of routines.

They take us on a stroll through their garden to enjoy their spring baskets.

Way too early for spring flowers here.

We share the daffodils we brought in for Easter.

We talk about kids, health, shopping, exercise, projects, politics – and laugh.

Good byes until the next time.

"Gosh, we miss you!"

Conversations with kids.

They tell us what's going on in their worlds.

Some are still working.

Some working from home.

Some not currently working.

One, along with her boy-friend, is recovering from the dreaded virus.

They each share how they're dealing with the isolation.

Some ask how we're doing.

Some think we're doing too much by being outside walking our rural neighborhood.

Some think it's great we're working on projects at the house.

None of them talk about what they (or we) will do when this is over.

"We love you, and we're concerned about you."

I hope to become a better "code reader."

Life Changes

Together, we'll get through this!
March/April 2020

Everything is a process.

Processes have invisible strands tying the pieces together. For me, the process started in the late spring of 2019. Spending 10 weeks in the southwest of Ireland and England left me shaken. The recognition of my materialism hit hard. The crazy pace of my life was revealed for what it was.

Crazy

I tried to share those revelations upon returning home.

My friends looked at me with the dazed look you give one when you think they've lost it. I still made little sense of this. I was trying to process it or figure out what it meant for me.

Another trip to Ireland in early 2020 reinforced these thoughts and cemented relationships there. I returned to my home in Colorado just as Covid-19 was being talked about prior to any lockdowns.

The lockdown gave me time and space to process those thoughts birthed in 2019. Granting me the opportunity to be at peace with experiencing a relaxed schedule. Provided opportunities to have communications with friends and family scattered around the globe and revealed the shared trauma of this pandemic.

No one wonders "why" someone is concerned at least not in my circle. It's my hope we will all come through this fear into love and thus come alive.

Come alive to the purposes created for each of us.

Ah, but first we have to recognize and acknowledge those purposes. I suspect the revelation process will be different for each of us. Some may even fight these truths preferring instead to return to what was. My pragmatic side knows this and thus expects the "coming through" will not necessarily allow us all to land in a "happy place".

There will be "happy places" but also some rough patches. There may be some friends cemented for life but also some lost. I hope to cling to the values I learned through this process, I aim to make them an integral part of me.

I hope more of us find the "happy place" and can affect and influence others still searching. I hope we can release some aspects of pre-pandemic life allowing them drift into what was, and thus allow those conditions to remain in the space of memory.

In Pandemic Lockdown

What I Mean...
...by what I say and what I do

When I get up and make your French press coffee,
I'm saying I love you.
When I sit beside you on the couch watching TV,
I'm saying I love you.
When I say, I'm okay with this isolation,
I'm saying my life was too busy,
I'm enjoying this break.
When I say, I'm frustrated about not getting my blood
work done,
I'm saying, I'm worried about the results of the labs.
When I cook new recipes,
I'm saying I want us to enjoy eating together.

Love and Trouble

Taking a sip from the glass on the dressing table
She inhaled deeply and let out a long, slow sigh.
Today was the day.
Dressed and ready, she would walk down the aisle.
She was radiantly beautiful.
Prince charming was standing at the front of the church.
Or was it prince charming?
She looked again.
Did she see a menacing grin and fangs?
The venue was filled.
People from her past, childhood, family and friends, they
were all there.
She looked again.
Still the menacing grin and fangs.
Would she?
Could she go through with this?
She didn't know…
But she couldn't walk away and leave all those guests
sitting there.
She sucked in another breath, more like a gasp, and started
the walk.
Perhaps slower than the music was paced.
She arrived, where his hand reached for hers.
He clutched it tightly and pulled her close.
The rest of the ceremony was a distant shadow receding
into her memory banks
Never to be recalled.
The reception was lively and the banquet hall was filled
With congratulatory statements and laughter.

Why did her heart feel so heavy?
Could she already foretell the misery to come?
He laughed as he moved around the room.
Everyone thought he was handsome and charming.
Friends commented on how fortunate she was…
The party ended late in the night.
A dark night.
They headed out of town on the back country road.
He was laughing and not watching the roadway.
There was a loud crash
As the car rammed into the old wooden bridge.
The vehicle careened over the banks where it submerged.
Its resting place, underwater.

Between Life and Death

Spring 2020

I cut my first
bunch of daffodils
before Easter.

It snowed during the night.
The blooms left for later
bent under the weight.
Buds not yet open
succumbed to the
morning snow.

My bunch of daffodils
in the living room
brought sunshine and the promise
of spring to come.
I've enjoyed this
bundle of blooms.
I've watched
the petals on these beautiful blooms
first become paper thin.
Still beautiful,
but the truth
of their fragility
is now evident.

A few more days
and the edges of those paper blooms
are dry and wrinkled,
some have turned a darker color,
others just became more fragile.

How like us.
We bud and bloom,
bringing sunshine and promise
to those around us.
Our lives bring beauty to some.
Like these blossoms,
we don't even recognize
the gradual process
of becoming more fragile.
Our bones are
more brittle,
muscle strength
steadily disappears,
our skin becomes
more translucent,
and our hair thins.

Like my daffodils,
we often fail
to recognize
these changes until
something happens.

Last night brought one
of those happenings.
I feel like
I should howl
and be in dissent.
Today, I'm weary and wonder,
what is this time all about?

Easter Dinner

Though grocery shopping was done yesterday, we failed to consider Sunday was Easter. What were we going to fix for Easter dinner? After discussing the menu, another trip to the store was in order. Two trips in one week? That's novel, especially during this time.

Holiday meals are always special. We usually invite company. The few times we've celebrated a holiday alone, they are still enjoyable and distinctive. It won't be different on Sunday, even though it will be a meal for the two of us.

What I read reminded me of preparations for a huge meal; the anticipation of interactions; the labor of love involved in creating whatever culinary delight fits the occasion; and the underlying tension between families, of how the distinct personalities interact, or what they may bring out in one another.

Dinner for two eliminates some tensions, but makes me wonder should I use the china? Should I get dressed up?

An overwhelming sense of lethargy seems to be upon me. No other pressing commitments are clamoring for my time. Why does fixing dinner sound exhausting? Has this weariness arrived on the wings of the grey clouds filling the sky outside my windows? Sunday predicts snow. My few early daffodils will shudder at the cold and then appreciate the moisture as the sun comes out and melts this white blanket.

How silly! I never have to prepare a holiday meal alone. These dinners are a collaborative event with hubby and I sharing the kitchen.

I long for spring!

Ordinary Things - The Kitchen Table

A cup of hot tea in my long thin pottery mug
warming my hands on a chilly morning
This my sense of grounding for any morning
or my release as the day ends
Simple comfort

The "picture" window in my living room
No not the normal description of a picture window
Just a rectangular window on the same wall as the front
door
Small
not fitting the description of a "picture" window
We snapped photos of the house when we hunted a new
abode
Back home reviewing photos I sighed and said
Too bad they'll be taking the picture with them when they
move
Hubby looked at the photo and laughed
A wonderful photograph
and the picture on the wall remains
It's a window
We have laughed at how sitting in the living room
the view from the window changes and reminds one of a
beautiful picture
Visitors at the house have suggested it is a picture as well
Simple pleasure

The table once recovered from my grandparent's basement
refinished and placed in my first apartment

The table which was their first kitchen table, albeit second-
hand
became my first table and remained so for years
Later on a side table in a large bedroom
The table now sits in our small apartment
and the guest there uses it as her kitchen table
The plan for the table to be gifted
to one of our grandchildren who treasures family history
It will be her table
The finish has changed multiple time
In doing so, have the stories it knows been removed or
rubbed out?
I think NOT
The table has had many homes
Wisconsin
Tennessee
Germany
North Carolina
Alabama
Tennessee again
Germany again
Maryland
Wisconsin again
Colorado
California
The granddaughter takes it back to Wisconsin

The history will continue with her
The table holds memories of meals shared
Cooking delights and early disasters
Babies being cuddled
Children learning to feed themselves
Tea-time with girlfriends and stories shared
Writing time before computers simplified the process
Family fights that wrought destruction
A place holder for a special antique
gracing a living space
Back again to being a kitchen table

If it could talk
what would it share
What wisdom would it dispel
This table does not look special
Many were produced in years past
and abound in used furniture stores
Almost given away
they are so common
But this table is NOT common to me
For me it holds roots
Confirms the roots I share with my grandparents
with their life struggles
faith and love
Roots I've planted in my children and grandchildren
Roots, I hope, are passed on to those future generations
Simple history—Simple love.

Time

The sun comes up
The sun goes down
Another day
Another night
So we count time

Covid-19 hit

Time stopped
I cook
I read
I write
I do creative things
I connect with others

According to the calendar
It's April
Really
Did the sun rise and set so many times

Time
There is no rush
No rush to fix or finish meal
No rush to arrive somewhere on time
Slowly work on projects
No rush to finish them

The sun comes up
Prepare morning drinks and luxuriate
My husband and I sit and chat
Enjoy the morning sky
With clouds drifting by
Notice the neighbors who walk their dogs
Listen to the increasing population of birds
Arriving for the season
Open patio doors to breathe in the cool
Fresh mountain air

Another cup of tea
Snuggle into a chair by the window
Allow the sun to warm my body
Get lost at this juncture
Reading
Writing
Communicating with another sheltering in her home
Spend time on one of those creative endeavors

Fix dinner
Enjoy the quiet of the night
The sun goes down

The Color of the Sky and other Natural Wonders

When we decided Colorado would be our new home, the color of the sky captivated me. For those who live in this location, you may be unaware many do not enjoy the intense blue colors we experience here. As a child, I would draw pictures, and the sky was *always* blue, a deep intense blue. I grew up in southern Wisconsin and the only month one consistently sees this blue is October. Blue may show in the morning, but by mid-morning the skies are frequently blue-grey color, or simply grey. The blue so clear in the skies of Colorado captivates me! I knew I would love this aspect of living here.

I stood on the shore of the lake we called home, loving the way my hair blew back as the wind whipped through the air, I said my silent prayers of "thanks" for the years I got to live here, listening to the waves either rolling or crashing on the shoreline; for the wind, the wild, crazy wind which blew across the lake, churning the waves into a frenzy. I said my "thanks" and admitted I would miss the wind.

We moved and settled into our new home. Surprise of surprises! Summer came, and so did the wind. I can expect a consistently intense wind at my home almost any summer day, sometime between 11 and 1. Winter wind also visits our property.

Summer and the wind will come, but before it arrives, I get to expect, then appreciate and enjoy the daffodils and lilacs spilling their colors onto the otherwise grey palette of early spring. It's coming! The buds are large and ready to burst. I'm ready to enjoy these visual delicacies.

Each season brings something special.

Moments

Moments run together
forming a day
a week
a month
a year
ultimately a life
The pause caused by Covid-19
has changed these moments

Moments are quieter
more peaceful
and sweeter
We make our morning brew
When the suns shines
we head out
Mugs
book in hand
Seated on the deck
We read
we talk
we enjoy our beverages of choice
Then we bask in the sun
We gaze upon the land
Enjoy the wildlife moving about us
Most often we marvel at the skies
the eagles
the clouds
the endless blue of Colorado skies

From our perch high on the hill
we watch neighbors out walking their dogs
The walkers and us
exchange waves
Invariably as the morning moves into mid-day
the wind picks up as we gather our things to return inside

These moments of quietness
and companionship are rich
They feed my soul
make me feel secure and comfortable
When the pandemic has run its course
what will I keep from these moments
How will these moments
merge with the others to define my life
There are plenty of moments
I'm enjoying and hoping to carry into my future
Will they change me
I've become protective of moments
not looking forward to when our activity may be busy
and we each awaken and spend a few minutes together
before heading off to accomplish different things
Only to show up together again at the day's end.

Faith

Wheels rolling down the road
Been this way before
Sights zip past the windows

Feelings jumbled
Uncertainties abound
COVID rampant
Political dissent unprecedented in my lifetime
Fear resides just below the surface
It hangs in the air around people
Health
Fear
Relational longings
Holiday uncertainties
Questionable financial futures
Partisanship canyon enlarges
Tolerance diminishes
Communication breaks down
Irrational choices fill the gap

Some pull inward
Some prepare to attack
I know not what to expect

Yet
God is my rock in these shifting times
Whatever is blown away
He will remain
My faith…

Violence in America

Words are weak. Words are inadequate. Writers often only have words to make sense of things.

These days are overwhelming, in many diverse ways. Things are out of control.

My heart hurts for our country. I feel like we've lost our way–or perhaps we smugly thought we "had" the way. We certainly tried to convince others of this.

Saturday, I Face-Timed with a friend from England. We lamented what's going on. She apologized, then told me she was glad she did not live here. I said, sometimes I wish I didn't live here.

The virus has been difficult for many. After last weekend's activities, things have become difficult for all throughout this country. No matter the color of your skin, can you honestly watch brutality and think it's okay? These events have challenged many of my thoughts. My parents brought me up to believe if you worked hard, you could accomplish anything. I believed this and thought the same opportunities were available to others. No one told me there was a racial component to this statement.

Those realities make me sad and make me want to cry.

I don't believe brutality or violence is going to change the problems we are experiencing. It doesn't help when the message from the bully pit is divisive. The churches I'm connected with are preaching a message of "Love

God, Love People." The message suggests to really love people means being able to extend love to those who make you feel uncomfortable. It encompasses much more than being non-violent, or thinking I can love everyone, but it's about me reaching out, one person to another one person at a time, no matter how different from me this person is.

What does it take for individuals to realize no matter what your appearance on the outside, we're each essentially created alike; with similar hopes, dreams, and desires for our future and for our children.

Change starts in the individual heart. As Americans, can we muster such a change, or have we become so hardened, so callous and so selfish to believe "me" is the force ruling the universe? The violence has brought issues to the forefront. I don't believe the violence will resolve the problem.

I'm kind of a nomad, believing things happen one step at a time. We entered this awful place with a lot of steps. We've got to get out of it with steps in a different direction.

So, instead of violence; instead of brutality, can we each commit to changing our own hearts, to doing simple acts of kindness for another who is radically different from ourselves?

Pandemic Waiting

Lucinda stood in her dining room looking around. Life was on "pause," due to the Corvid-19 virus. She thought she'd adjusted to the social distancing and isolation requested by the government to slow the spread of the dreaded disease. Why was it considered "dreaded?" Could it be "dreaded" because it developed out of nowhere, and then rapidly spread to everywhere? She and Scotty were adjusting. The pantry was stocked; they were working on some projects; technology allowed them to remain connected to family and friends scattered around the globe; they enjoyed the peacefulness of where they lived. Well, they enjoyed a quiet peacefulness when the neighbor's dogs weren't incessantly barking. Many had complained about this neighborhood irritation.

It was a nice day, and Scotty thought he'd give one more try speaking with the neighbor about these critters of his, and about the value of neighborly relations. The neighbor had on at least two previous times acknowledged his dogs were poorly behaved.

Scotty drove his truck to their house. No dogs appeared as he ascended their driveway, and he thought this was unusual. Generally, anyone walking in the roadway brought the dogs charging down the driveway to the limits of their electric fence. From there, they continued barking and jumping until the pedestrians were out of sight. He figured they must be in the house. So, he got out of his truck and shut the vehicle door. Wham! The dogs appeared from the backside of the house and attacked him. The one lunged for his face. Scotty put up his arm to push the dog off. They were barking and Scotty was yelling. Both dogs were attacking Scotty when the owner came out.

Lucinda had limited knowledge of the conversation which ensued between the fellows, but later learned the neighbor was initially indignant and felt his dogs had every right to be aggressive. He expressed marginal interest in if there'd been any injury. He and Scotty talked and then Scotty came home. Lucinda's squeamish stomach almost turned at the sight of the injuries, and anger rose within her. Because of the pandemic, neither she nor Scotty felt comfortable heading to the Emergency Room. Fortunately, they knew an ER doc and Scotty talked with him on the phone. The doc relayed instructions for wound care. And so, the process began. They contacted the County Animal Control Authorities, who said they would be out in the morning. They sent photos of the injury sites to them, along with a written statement of the incident. Neither of them slept well during the night, Scotty in pain and Lucinda, angry. Lucinda spent the night thinking of ways to make her neighbors understand the severity of the situation. She wanted them to become responsible neighbors and dog owners and even thought of ways to eradicate the dogs. She wanted those dogs gone!

The next morning was busy. Lucinda recognized the foolishness of her previous night's thoughts and knew she would never act on her thoughts. Scotty received a call from the deputy at Animal Control; contacted the neighbor requesting immunization records for each of the dogs; contacted his own doctor, who set up an afternoon appointment. The neighbor provided the health records and inquired about the injuries, hoping Scotty would be ok. Animal Control met with him at our house before seeing the neighbor, then called later to provide an update. Between the two communications, Scotty learned there was a previous complaint about these dogs biting a delivery driver (but the home owner's association issued the complaint so it never resulted in court action); therefor their complaint was taken seriously because it was not the first one; it surprised the neighbor to learn there would be a court summons. Lucinda's concerns remained high for her husband. Many of the wounds were extremely deep and one, besides being deep, was a wide gash on the backside of his knee.

Since the visit from Animal Control, the dogs are noticeably absent outdoors. They are only visible when the owner is present. He disclosed they were making the necessary applications to have a fence installed. Scotty is on antibiotics to thwart off any infection. The wound sites are extremely sensitive and his leg frequently hurts. Both Lucinda and Scotty feel beaten down; their energy levels are low; their tolerance is reduced. Both are concerned about health issues which may arise from either the dog attack or the virus. Both question if there will be legal repercussions for the neighbor or if his connections within the legal community will provide immunity.

Wait is the verb for this season. Scotty and Lucinda *wait* to see how the wounds heal; *wait* to see if the legal system functions as it's supposed to, or if favoritism and nepotism prevails; *wait* for the Covid-19 virus to be behind us.

We will discover how imperfect things are after the *waiting* is done.

Garden Disparities

The garden I'm enjoying today is nothing like the one I own. Both houses sit atop a hill or on a ridge-line, but the similarities end there. The front of my house faces the roadway. The front door of this house faces the street, but the front of the house is the backside and it overlooks the hillside down with the ocean in the distance. My garden is wild and mostly untamed. Scattered Gamble Oak trees share the land with hundred-plus year old sage brush. When the sun bakes the morning dew or moisture from the sage and the breeze blows through, the pungent fragrance fills the air. Wild animals roam our land save for the small section we've fenced to keep out the larger wildlife. Even in this small space, efforts to cultivate anything edible are fraught with constant battles against the rodents and small creatures. I've almost given up thinking I can grow anything for the kitchen. Our garden, yard or property is rugged and displays the natural beauty of rural Rocky Mountain living. Our home provides ever changing weather and the full range of four seasons. Because of rural living and more spacing between homes, our environment is much quieter and darker, rendering the star filled night sky almost within reach.

This highly manicured garden thrives with each plant species selected for a designated purpose—some for shape, others for color, but each for a specific effect as the planted areas line the stairway down to the lower level guest house and pool area. Butterflies casually flit from plant to plant, while hummingbirds dance through the air, spotting the floral blooms. The area is alive with texture, shape and color, creating an atmosphere of lush coastal tranquility. The casual ocean breezes waft the essence of eucalyptus through the air. One level hosts an English cook's garden with pathways creating various shapes. Inside these garden shapes, plants are pruned to present different heights. Most any herb for culinary delights can be found in this area. Along the north side of the walkway and home is a raised bed, home to various succulents. The placement draws attention to the varied and unique shapes and sizes of these plants. This property provides an extensive visual paradise, offering a respite from months of sequestering in my home.

I feel extremely blessed to live where I do, and to have a nephew willing to share his home with its unique characteristics and features. Both nourish my soul.

Different Perspective on Aliens

The strange silver colored disk shape soared and twirled through the atmosphere. The device was small and fast, which made it difficult for other planetary monitoring devices to detect it. Upon closer examination, if one could get close enough, they would discover the shape appeared more like two cup saucers placed right sides together. An endless row of windows connected the two pieces of the saucer together. Yet no one was even aware it was in the sky, nor attempted to get close enough to observe it and so, undetected, this entity continued hurling itself through space.

If you looked inside, it might surprise you to find workspaces, countertops and machinery lining the perimeter of the saucer. In the central area were four cubical spaces. Two appeared to be sleeping chambers, which housed hammocks. One was like a kitchen and the fourth, it was an undetermined space. There were two rather long, lanky creatures, deep turquoise. They moved around the space, clicking and chirping back and forth. Occasionally, one would shake his head in either agreement or disagreement.

One turned to the other and said, "Finkler, we must speak English. We need to perfect our use of the language so we can communicate with the humanoids when we land."

Presumably Finkler sputtered out some chirps and shrill sounds before he said, "Ok, Bowler. It's a hard language, so I take longer to put my thoughts together. Our speech is easier. It's what we know, and so much of it is intuitive. But you win. I'll speak English."

"Thanks Finkler," said Bowler.

"We should put on those strange rubber suits so we can adjust to them also," said Finkler.

"Yes… we should. I've been avoiding doing so. They look hot, and will be tight. Do you think humanoids wear such things?" said Bowler.

They opened a cabinet and took out two matching purple jumpsuits with stockings attached. They shook the outfits, turned them in one direction, then another as they contemplated how to wear them. Finally, Finkler inserted his foot into the garment, searching for the leg, and pulled the item on.

"Awe! My feet don't fit in here."

Bowler replied, "I noticed that before. I suppose the design is to make us appear more like the humanoids. We can hide the digits on our feet, but our hands will be bare. Come on, let's pull these suits on. We must learn how to maneuver in them."

"Yeah. Just wait until you get into your suit," said Finkler, as he inserted his final arm and readjusted the neckline of his suit.

At that moment, one device on the counter emitted a high-pitched squeal. Finkler hit one lever at the control panel and the saucer seemed to hover, gently swaying from side to side. Bowler and Finkler each put on goggles which covered their forest green eyes and peered out the windows.

"We must have entered earth's galaxy when we put on these suits. I understand they call these things stars. They throw off such a white light against this dark navy backdrop. Can you spot the orb out there in space? It appears wrapped in a mist, giving off a soft light," said Bowler.

"Yup, that should be earth," said Finkler. He turned to Bowler and continued. "How do we find the house we identified as our target?"

"Slow down! Slow down! We have to slow down even more. Let's just coast for a few minutes," said Bowler.

The saucer speed reduced even more; again Bowler and Finkler gazed out the windows. The view was incredible. It was breathtaking for these two who have traveled through multiple galaxies. As they approached earth, it was not lengthy, just an orb, but they could catch the light reflecting over the curvature. Suddenly, colors appeared. The blues were much brighter than the navy from the dark skies; greens and browns covered much of the mass; solid white shone on two of the edges of the orb.

"Are those the polar ice caps we studied?" asked Bowler.

"Must be," said Finkler. He spun around to head back to the control panel. He started punching entries into a screen. "You sure about these coordinates? We don't want to land in the wrong place."

Bowler said, "I went over them multiple times. We watched the house and the humanoids living there. There are no four-legged creatures, only two humanoids.

"Ok. I slowed us down so we could better observe this system. I hope the inhabitants are receptive to us."

"Yes. Me too. We've got to find some system that will accept us. Life at home is deteriorating," said Bowler.

Finkler returned to one window, and the two continued to gaze in amazement at the views below them.

"Oh, I forgot. We need to turn on the cloaking device. We've reduced our speed and don't want to be picked up by any detection system," said Finkler.

"I'll take care of that," said Bowler.

"Done," said Bowler as he returned to the window.

As they viewed the topography, they talked about how some of what they saw was like their home. Yet it amazed them to see turbulent wind tossing tree tops back and forth. Trees were an unknown phenomenon to them and they didn't know what to call them.

Chimes sounded from the control panel.

"We're close," said Finkler. "But it's dark down there. We'll have to turn on the landing light to ensure we don't collide with anything."

Bowler said, "Ok, but postpone switching on the lights as long as possible."

No one in the neighborhood heard anything. Donald had his dogs out for the evening when he noticed this orange tunnel like glow shine in his neighbor's back yard. Then he saw nothing. He returned to his house shaking his head, wondering what he saw, or if he just had too much wine after dinner.

Bill and Sue were just shutting blinds and getting ready to call it a night when they also saw the orange tunnel like glow highlighting a circular spot in their backyard. Suddenly, the light vanished. In the glimmering moonlight, they could discern the shadow of a saucer-like shape. And then, just as quickly, it disappeared. All was quiet outside, but they weren't comfortable with what they had witnessed.

Bill grabbed a flashlight from under the kitchen sink and met Sue at the backdoor. They turned on the outside light. Precisely when they opened the backdoor, they saw these turquoise and purple things walk around their backyard. Sue clutched Bill's arm as she let out a small scream.

"Shush," said Bill.

"Hello," said one creature. "We are friendly. We mean you no harm."

"Why are you here?" said Bill.

"We want to meet and learn about people from earth. We want to understand your land. Do you mind if we remain here for several days? We won't bother you and will only talk with you when you are ready. But we would like to sit with you and talk while we're here."

"Sure, but it's late tonight. Can we chat in the morning over breakfast?" said Bill.

"Great."

They exchanged good night greetings before Bill and Sue returned to the house.

"Can you believe what just happened? We had aliens or something land in our backyard and talk with us! Are you okay making breakfast tomorrow morning?" asked Bill.

Sue said, "Sure. What do you expect they want to discuss with us?"

"I don't know, but we'll soon find out."

The next couple of days passed quickly. Bill and Sue learned their alien guests were Finkler and Bowler. The four interacted together easily. Sue and Bill learned their people sent them into space to find a planet which might be hospitable to their race. Their planet was losing resources and would not support the race much longer.

Donald called one morning to say he had witnessed something turquoise and purple in their backyard. Bill tried to calm his anxieties, but when he threatened to call the authorities, Bill and Susan met with Finkler and Bowler and told them it was best they leave. They did, and now Susan and Bill sit around and wonder if they'll ever see Bowler and Fincler again.

Susan frequently ponders their visit. Her mind returns to time spent with them and wonders if they return, will they find her house again.

She replays the conversation with Donald when she told him, You are angry because I invited the aliens to breakfast. You considered them dangerous. Ha! They landed in my backyard not yours.

Susan struggled with Donald. She blamed him for Bowler and Finkler leaving. She remembered telling him. You're just angry they didn't land in your yard and didn't have breakfast with you. What would you have served them, anyway? We enjoyed waffles and fresh fruit. They marveled at the coffee. There's nothing like it on their planet.

She thought about how hard she tried not to stare at their turquoise skin and the slits that revealed their forest green eyes. There were two of them. Their noses appeared flat. She assumed those were their noses. Their mouths were small and didn't open very wide.

The four of them casually talked about the differences between their lives.

They spoke English clearly and said they've been studying it for years. They explained "years" as the word we humans use, but in actuality, it was a flash in time.

Both Susan and Bill struggled to understand what they meant and how long they had studied. Several times they made these chirping noises and suddenly something like a giggle. They never clarified their communications with each other, so part of Susan questioned if she was in danger. They may have sensed those feelings as they quickly interjected a statement thanking her for her hospitality, or questioning her about the purpose of some item within the house.

They said they've heard humans have tender hearts and want to study the limits of that tenderness.

They thought being invited in to share a meal displayed tenderness. It surprised them at the effortless way Susan put together the meal; at the fragrances emitting from the kitchen; at how cold and juicy strawberries were. It surprised Susan at how they slurped the food in. She couldn't discern if they even chewed it.

Susan tried to keep the wonder from her face, as she didn't want to startle them.

She asked if they landed by chance in her yard?

No, we've been observing this place called earth, and pre-selected this location.

She wanted to know how long have they been studying she and Bill?

Susan found this disconcerting. Knowing some outside force or being had been watching she and Bill then later selected landing here.

She didn't think of herself being tender. She tried to be compassionate towards others. But thought, if they've been watching her, they are aware there are times that isn't possible. Sometimes she had no patience.

The Washing Machine

Is Covid-19 the reason? Is it because of the extended absence of social interactions? Am I befuddled because of the reality of my mother's impending death? Is this unease the result of something I'm unaware of?

A decision is pending…

I feel the contents of my brain have been dumped into a washing machine for a thorough cleaning. This machine isn't an energy efficient front loader which takes the laundry and gently rolls it one direction and then the other so the water flows through the fabric, and as it drains from the machine, the dirt leaves with it.

No, my thoughts dropped into a heavy duty, high agitation machine. Once the water enters the machine, the mechanism sharply whips from left to right, forcefully twisting the drum contents back and forth. The end goal remains the same: the dirt drains out with the water after a wickedly fast spin.

I'm in the middle of the high agitation cycle. Thoughts are colliding and crashing against one another. A decision is awaiting the sorting of these thoughts. The process is unpleasant, and uncomfortable for me. My normal demeanor allows me more confidence about pending decisions. Or perhaps I allow myself time to process the thoughts so I can be comfortable and thus be confident.

Momentary revelation, previous decision junctions were washed through the front loader machine with a more gentle process than the current state where I find myself.

Conflicting thoughts are crashing against one another. How long was the wash cycle set for? When the muck drains with the grimy water, what thoughts will remain with me? Will I have an answer to the looming question?

My House

…sits high above the road, with peaked ceilings and lots of windows which allow the sky to enter and be part of my daily life. That could mean blue skies with white clouds, or grey skies with dark angry clouds waiting to dump something on me. Some days, it simply means living in a cloud with little ability to see beyond the windows. Cloudless nights are the best when the stars are sparkling against the navy background, appearing so close I think I can reach out to grab a couple just for me.

I have filled my house with unique aromas the last two weeks as I've given my creative side freedom to explore recipes from a Turkish cookbook given to me by a friend before she departed this valley I now call home. Distinct aromas and unique flavors from combinations of spices I've seldom used before. I never knew how much dill changes the flavor of beef; or tomatoes when skinned and de-seeded, then cooked with stock, have a less acidic taste. These flavors are different and fun from how I normally cook—not strong or spicy hot, just different. We've found the food to be hearty and very filling. The cooking has been an adventure, but also exhausting. Most of the meals are labor intensive in their preparation. I now understand how these dishes are prepared to honor guests. So I can say, I've been honoring my husband, honoring us, honoring how we have one another to share this time with. I may have one more Turkish meal in me for this season, afterwards the book will go back on the shelf and I'll return to meals and culinary delights we've enjoyed at different times or try something completely different.

I walk the switch back driveway down to our mailbox where remnants of last year's dead grasses and the sagebrush are still moist from the night's snow. The fragrance of sage hits me and reminds me of first moving here eight years ago and the wonder I experienced the first time I opened the door and smelled sage. I was so surprised and then surprised I hadn't expected this. Our property sits on hundred-year-old sage plants. How could I expect to be surrounded by sage and yet not smell it? The pleasure of this aroma and memories of my naivety bring a smile to my face and are part of what contributes to making me feel safe at home.

I savor the simple pleasures. It's a way to keep the pandemic at arm's length from me. To date, we personally know of no one who's succumbed to the virus. Part of me wonders how long I will keep this truth, and I push those thoughts away. I'm aware each of us, collectively everyone, is touched by this pandemic and the effects will be deep and far reaching. I push away the thoughts about how long it will be before we return to our normal activities.

I push away…

The Threat to Us

I sit here at my computer, knowing deep in my heart how fortunate I am, very fortunate, to live where I do. Nestled in my house, gazing through the window at the landscape before me, with much more than the prescribed distance between myself and my neighbors. In many ways, the pandemic feels surreal to me.

Below the surface of this peace lies the uncertainty of what's coming. Not just the health uncertainties. It's an uncertainty which is larger than me, an uncertainty for family and friends living around the country and in Europe. Southwestern rural Ireland is a fantasy destination for tourists. The Irish play to this role well, as they know their livelihood depends upon it. Many are my friends. I write with them; I worship with them; we eat together, go on walks or shopping outings—not as a tourist, but being one with them. They are just like me, carrying hopes and dreams for the future and their children; concerns and fears for those they love; and memories and hurts from their past they are trying to heal or run from. They have captivated my heart.

Tourist season should start there, but their borders are closed. With travelers unwelcome, and only essential businesses open, the residents of the Republic of Ireland find themselves restricted to home and the distance they can travel from their home. In some ways, it sounds like here, doesn't it?

The other day I read a headline in the Telegraph (UK version) that said something like: Forget about your bucket list of vacation plans. It hit me hard as I thought about my friends. Then reality struck me. Not only Ireland but also the valley where I live. As a country, family and friends will face hardship.

Strange how we compartmentalize things. Right now, health is on one level. Providing shelter and food for the family is another level. After the pandemic subsides and we're working on creating our new normal, what will our focus be? We'll each need to identify the new me and the collective us. Who will we be? Will health, shelter and food still be priorities? Then there is all the other stuff. Yes, I said STUFF. How will people respond to that? How much do we need? Will individuals return to clamoring for material things, or recognize after a certain level of acquisitions, the stuff is a burden? Will the concern people developed for others be part of their new normal? Will we have more compassion for others or return to clamoring to gain more? Who will I be after I survive the pandemic? Who will you be?

Special Place

The local coffee shop (which shall remain nameless) is one of my favorite places, as it is for many of the valley residents. There's no one special thing which happened there, but instead I've had many special meetings and connections with others there. The walls have heard many serious conversations; funny conversations; quiet times between lovers; or witnessing patrons there to read the local papers or work on their laptops while enjoying a cup of brew.

Even before entering the building, the fragrance of strong coffee wafts through the door. I think it actually seeps out of the walls and fills the air. Upon departing, you will drop the essence of this fragrance wherever you go. The floor is wooden and beat-up, reminiscent of an old warehouse. In one wall is an ancient lift used for moving supplies up and down, now displaying a piece of rustic art. The shop owners covered the wainscoted walls with local art. All except for the large bulletin board, which shouts out activities happening within the locality. Several quiet corners offer space for intimate conversations, yet the energy in this place is electric. A buzz fills the air. Some generated from patrons having conversations, some from background music and some from the whiz and whir of various machines at the coffee bar.

Everyone in town knows this place. Since the shelter-in-place orders, this coffee shop only provides carry-out orders. I suspect the bustling activity has changed. I've not entered the café, though I have enjoyed a brew from there several times after my hubby ran in and got two cups.

As much as I enjoy this establishment, staying home hasn't been a sacrifice. We've taken to making our drink of choice here in our own kitchen, and then enjoying the brew either on the deck or inside. We don't finish up this time with our clothing drenched in the smell of coffee. The space at home is quieter, and our conversations flow in any direction—and often do. This morning-time has become more contemplative and we explore different feelings about what is happening. I believe I may have become less extroverted during this time, and I'm okay with that.

What's Different

My calendar used to identify tasks which kept me busy most of the week. I'd awaken to the fresh mountain morning, but not ponder it for long before heading down to breakfast drinks and a study with my hubby. Then we'd be off to …wherever.

Now, I've become a sloth. (Except for two early morning online meetings.) Sleeping with no concern for time, awakening when my body is ready. I awaken to the same fresh mountain morning air, but take time to ponder the coolness and how fresh it both feels and smells. If hubby is still sleeping, I creep downstairs to spend some time either writing or reading. I'm grateful for every quiet moment, which was mostly absent from my "before the pause" story.

Spring has arrived with the promise of summer heat soon to follow. I savor the lingering daffodils who are hanging on for a peek at the soon to bloom lilacs. If they look closely, they'll see the Bridal Wreath is abloom as well. Poppies are waving their bright colors to me from the deck as I walk past the patio doors. They are unaware the season's tomato plants will soon join them, which I will endeavor to cultivate for "us", and not the chipmunks.

For me, this season of "pause" has proved refreshing and relaxing. It's been healthy for my body and my soul. I've slowed down to view and then reflect on the beauty which surrounds me. There is time for me to reflect on my thoughts. I feel peace in knowing my schedule is mine, not the result of me thinking I need to, or am expected to, do "something."

My peaceful moments are interrupted, especially when I read news as it relates to travel. Travel and my life are interwoven and will certainly change. I'll have no control or choices about the changes imposed. How will we continue our outreach work in Ireland? Travel within the US, I expect more will be by auto, but overseas? YIKES! So I push the thoughts away. It isn't an option yet. I have no control over the decisions and they don't affect today.

Push the thoughts away…

So, instead, I'll ponder how the oaks are growing, the pollen heads exploding and the leaves getting larger. My lavender plants are showing early signs of growth. I'll rejoice at my Lamb's Leaf lettuce breaking forth with its tiny pearl shaped leaves and wait in anticipation of the crop to come.

I'll wait inside before I open my door to reenter the world and enjoy this season for at least a little longer.

Circle of Life

The blooms are breaking forth
Hummingbirds and bees swarm the yellow flowers
Green leaves shriveling and giving up their life blood
Soon the flowers will produce seeds as the plant withers
and dies

My front row seat to this miracle of nature fascinates me
Our blue agave bloom process took longer than
research suggested
The show has been fun
Gardner friends encourage us to cut back the leaves
As their nourishment drains
The outer skin will shrivel and harden

As it is said
   the curtain closes on this performance

Recognition of the Unknown

The Recognition of All the Things I Don't Know
My list keeps getting longer
How about yours

The first revelation was after having kids
then all the years of raising them

I assumed I had a solid understanding of who my mom
was
and why she acted as she did
Those beliefs were upended
I saw her in a different light
which allowed me to appreciate her as a woman
A woman who was kind and caring
She became my friend
and I enjoyed a great relationship with her

Another revelation after my marriage fell apart
was you can't change or control another
or even circumstances
Wow
This created an opportunity for personal growth
revealing much I didn't know

I learned a lot about myself previously unknown
The door opening to this lengthy pathway
still leads me on
I may never reach the final destination

I keep learning more about myself
Some days I look at those revelations
and wish to change them
Other days I am surprised
by the truths revealed

My deep passion about individuals and culture
also revealed another pathway
into this land of all the things I didn't know

This writing was to be about landing
I'm not sure I'll ever land in this life

One significant lesson learned
while discovering all the things I didn't know is
my quest continues for as long as I'm alive

The more I learn about myself
the more individuals I meet
the deeper my friendships become
and the more life I experience
the more I find I don't know
Mostly this fills me with wonder

Many times something new is birthed within me
be it more curiosity
greater compassion
deeper love
more appreciation for life
Other times
I'm saddened by the human condition

So life
bring it on
Keep showing me
all the things I didn't know

I'll keep absorbing those truths into who I am
I suspect these truths will spill out
into my writing
and the life I share with others

But please don't expect me
to *land*
as long as I have breath
within me

Without Substance

The marine layer rose from the sea and rolled onto the
land
Enveloping all which hindered its progression inland

Standing on the patio deck I watched
the advancing wall of grey coming closer

Almost like an eraser
removing all else from view
Still, I stood

Before long I found myself shrouded within the grey

Slowly, my eyes adjusted
to this colorless world

But not my mind

My world is full of color

How can this be

The thought
just relax and let it flow
entered my mind

I stopped fighting the loss of color

Instantly I found myself in an unfamiliar world
one filled with shadows and shapes
which formed and drifted past me

I reached out to touch something
appearing similar to a lily pad bloom
but it had no substance
my hand went straight through it

I swung around and peered at where the house existed

It was becoming grey and obscure

The ground below me became less stable and my own
body felt formless

What is happening to the world I thought I knew

Stuck in the Muck

That's where I'd say I am right now
Try as I might
I can't get out

Life is calling to me
Wanting to move forward
Into the future

I am stuck

Wanting to say good-bye

Needing closure
Which comes from tradition
Of family and friends
Sharing stories of a loved one

The date not yet set

Miles between all the parties
Feels perceived as disinterest

Words don't bridge the gap
To understanding

Motivation for others
Is different

Linda L Flynn

My head tells me to accept the situation
And to move on

My heart is heavy
And the weight drops
To my boots

I'm stuck in the muck

Roots and Wings

Words on paper absorbed in mind creates images
Brings to life other places and times

Roots and wings intermingle
Twisting and growing together

Each attempting to be dominant

The one who planted words and dreams had deep roots
and has left the earth

Yet she birthed one with wings

Did she know what she planted

Do any of us

She marveled as she watched the wings grow and
develop

Did she know she was appreciated and loved

Mothers

We each have a mother until the day we don't.

How such news hits us is individual and different for all.

It happened to me on August 12, 2020. Intellectually, we all know death comes, yet I was unprepared for the feelings unleashed within myself. My mother birthed an independent child. She gave me wings to fly and encouraged me on my many and varied adventures. Her death has made the ground seem a little less solid. I'm not ready to be the eldest female in my core family. I feel the emptiness of not being able to pick up the phone and share the plan for my next exploit. She wasn't there to celebrate my latest accomplishment.

Because of her health conditions I haven't been able to share these types of events with her for several years. Yet now, a vacuum resides within me which I didn't know before.

I replay memories of the lady who enjoyed laughing, and when she laughed, she filled the room with joy. One of her "love languages" was acts of service. Her tender and compassionate heart frequently reached out to others who were older than she, or in need of assistance. One would find her washing dishes at someone's house, or pulling weeds when she came to visit you. Careful and deliberate selection went into the gifts and cards she sent to others. If you ever received one of her cards, you would think someone wrote it just for you. I've been reading some of her cards and letters sent to me and can see ways she vicariously shared my adventures. As a mother myself, I recognize this trait as I too have lived through some of my daughters' adventures through imagined participation in their experience while admiring how brave they are.

She loved nature and the sights of wild animals. I remember when she started wearing blue jeans and first learned to ride a horse. Those outdoor activities gave her great pleasure. And it made me happy to watch her experiencing new undertakings.

She, like her mother before her, was a splendid cook; fed her family well; enjoyed trying new recipes and had a bountiful harvest from her garden of vegetables and flowers. Her daughters and grand-daughters also inherited this love of cooking. The gardening skills didn't land in my direction, though I enjoy a vase of fresh flowers any day.

Pondering these recollections generates feelings of great happiness and intense sadness.

For the time being, I see myself using lots of tissues.

Watch Your Mind

Watch your mind... As individuals, we tend to forget the power of the mind, and forget the power we can exercise over the mind.

Watch your mind... What lessons there are to learn? The past creeps in and tries to steal the peace we've learned to live with, replacing it instead with memories of pain and heartache.

Oh, watch your mind... You can command those thoughts to depart and instead focus on positive or joyful thoughts for today. There is beauty which exists around us. If we take occasion to search for it, we'll find it. It may be as grand as the sky lit up with the radiant colors of the sun saying goodbye at day's end, or as small as a perfect flax flower with its open head waving in the morning sunshine. Beauty abounds.

Watch your mind... No lectures, no speeches, no judgment—instead, allow forgiveness and acceptance to flow through you to those around you. Share the joy of living with those you come in contact with. Speak words of encouragement and life to others. Let your words tell others who they can be. Speak life!

Weren't We Beautiful

Yes, we were. We were so full of ourselves and confident we knew about life. It was a grand time! Then we started having children. At the beginning, that didn't diminish our beauty. We still glowed. And, yes, we each have mental images locked away, from an era when a perfect photo captured all our beauty, elegance and light.

We didn't realize how silently those traits drifted away. Raising kids, relationship issues, work stressors, extended family tensions all placed expectations upon us. As women, many of us assumed we had to meet those juxtaposed expectations and took them on, unaware of how they weighed us down and started deconstructing the women we were.

Life continued, and at some turning point, we rebelled at the presumption we could meet all those needs.

When the weight of those shackles lifted, time began a miraculous healing process. A unique beauty emerged. Look at those images. There's more joy, more peace, more acceptance and grace.

Yes, Aren't We Beautiful?

Autumn Musings

The gradual palette change erupted into full color. Autumn arrived in all its glory. It was grand. Just as the crickets have been saying, the winds blew in the reminder "winter's coming." The winds have been wild and raging. They stripped the tapestry from many trees as they whipped through the valley and the countryside. The parched land is now littered with the remnants of the tree's clothing.

This change brought relief from the high temperatures endured during the summer. Looking at the fields, the land is parched and dry. Grasses reflect burnt umber, the pine trees cling to their evergreen hew all against the deep blue of the sky.

I drive to town, soaking in the beauty of this transition. The mountain is devoid of its beloved snowcap. I'll hold tight to these images. Fall is my ultimate favorite season. I embrace it wherever I live. Many tell me they have a love hate relationship with this season. They love the way it looks and hate it reminds them of winter to follow. For me, what follows has never affected my feelings about autumn. Because it's so dry here, fire danger remains high. Hopefully, winter and snow will come to refresh and restore the land to prepare for spring.

The Hotel

Sheila and Ed escaped their busy life in the city for a weekend in a tiny mountain town. This remote little burg was home to a historic hotel. After reading about the establishment in a travel magazine they determined it was somewhere they wanted to visit.

Arriving late in the afternoon, the clean environment of the town showcased it's many historic features. Most storefronts contained full window displays, yet none of the shops appeared open. But no worries. They were on a mission; they wanted to get checked into their hotel, settle in their room and make their weekend plans.

The hotel was a grand, albeit old, structure situated downtown on Main Street. It was the only three story building in town. Raging River had been a renowned gold mining town back in the day. However, after gold went bust, many miners moved further west, hoping to make their riches with the silver ore they heard was on the other side of the mountain range. Some women and older folks remained in the town. A schoolhouse and church survived in town for those who stayed behind. Over time, ruffians took control of Raging River forcing many of those who had remained to return east to more civilized cities. As settlers continued to travel west, people stopped in town to purchase supplies and get information. The fever of getting rich with gold or silver reached epidemic proportions.

Mines began to dry up. Those who had frequented Raging River for supplies or to retrieve their mail stopped appearing. Law and order eventually came to the west and gunslingers were no longer welcome in town. Things changed. No one knows how the hotel survived, but people continue to come stay there and walk the dusty streets, peering into the storefronts on Main Street. A few rustic homes lined the streets off the main drag, most with front porches piled high with split wood as proof the inhabitants are prepared for a frigid winter. The hotel, restaurant, gas station, a cafe and a small quick shop are the only remnants remaining of the once thriving town.

Because of the elevation, Sheila and Ed arrived breathlessly at the hotel front desk. They gazed around. The woodwork was thick and dark, much of it carved. Behind the desk clerk was an old board with pegs, room numbers and keys.

"Well, howdy! You folks checking in for the night or longer?"

Ed said, "We're here for the weekend. We're the Slingers."

"Ah, yes. I see your reservation here. Please sign the register. I have you at the top of the stairs in room 201. Just call the front desk if you need anything. We serve dinner in the dining room from 6 to 8. And breakfast starts at 7."

They collected their luggage, climbed the staircase and discovered room 201 at the top of the landing, as the clerk had said. Ed inserted the old key into the lock and heard the screeches as the innards strained to unlock the door.

The door squealed as they opened it.

"Wonder why the maintenance man doesn't oil the hinges," said Ed.

Sheila walked into the room, dropped her suitcase on the floor, and headed directly to the window. A gentle breeze was blowing the white muslin curtains into the room.

"Ed, come here. We have an amazing view of the street and some houses hidden from the main road."

The town appeared picturesque, and the houses looked like children playing some sort of game had randomly scattered them on the hillside. The road was not straight, but curved up a steep hill.

"Sheila, did you look up the other hill?"

"No, the town and the tiny houses mesmerized me," said Sheila.

"Look. Look. The mine is on the hill. Remnants of train rails are visible near what appears to be the entrance to the mine. In fact, there's an old mining cart sitting on the hillside. I can't believe there isn't still some gold in those hills."

Shelia shook her head. "None of that silly dreaming. We're here for us. Remember? We plan to explore an old town and hike forest trails. I don't want to get bitten by the gold fever bug."

"Uh-huh," said Ed.

Sheila shrugged, and said, "Yeah. I know you. Hey. Let's change clothes and head down for dinner."

"Excellent idea. I'm starved."

The dining room, dimly lit by tall candles and several wall mounted oil lamps, was filled with a mismatch of old wooden tables, all sporting brightly colored starched tablecloths. Wood lay in the grate of the enormous fireplace, ready to be lit if the evening became cool. Two other couples occupied tables in opposite corners of the room. Staff directed Sheila and Ed to a window table where they were seated, and handed each a leather-bound menu. Many of the items on the menu were local which was comprised of wild game, fresh vegetable dishes, decadent sounding desserts paired with dessert coffees. Yum! Everything appeared enticing. They ordered, then sat back to enjoy the recommended bottle of Pinot Grigio as they gazed out the window. The day's light waned and the old gas streetlights shed a soft glow against the evening light. Someone lit the fire. Before long the sounds of cracks and pops could be heard emitting from the fireplace.

Sheila peered at the business across from the hotel. This store was lit up. She was sure when they walked through town it appeared shuttered with just window displays from times past, like so many other buildings. Yet tonight, the shop was lit. She could see four musicians in the back corner, three guys and one woman. All dressed in old western style attire. The musicians played, yet no one else was visible in the building. Several glasses of water sat on the counter.

Sheila frowned, and Ed said, "Are you all right? I thought you were excited about having dinner in the hotel."

"I am. Sorry. Do you see the shop over there?"

"Uh-Huh. Why?"

"It seems so strange. I was sure it was a vacant building with just store front window displays when we walked by earlier today. Now the lights are on. There appear to be four musicians playing in there, but no one else."

"Maybe they practice and jam there. I see the wait staff bringing our entrees. Let's enjoy our dinner."

The food was exquisite. The atmosphere was peaceful. Soft music played in the background. Both Sheila and Ed relaxed; glad to escape home and all the responsibilities there. They laughed as they planned and schemed the events for the rest of their holiday weekend.

Periodically Sheila glanced out the window, and Ed said, "Hey. I'm here. Would you mind rejoining me?"

She'd laugh and say, "Sure. Here I am."

"Sure you are. That's why you keep gawking out the window. Tell you what. You focus on us, here, now. After we finish dinner, we'll walk over so you can look in the window."

"Oh Ed. Thanks. I'd like that."

They finished their dinner, dessert and wine; paid their bill and hand-in-hand walked out into the street.

The street was dimly lit and deserted, save for the couple advancing from the opposite direction. Sheila and Ed paused, watching this couple as they approached the storefront, stopped in front of the door, reached for the handle and pushed open the door. As they stepped across the threshold, their blue jeans and plaid shirts transformed into old period style western clothing. The transformation included all details. Even the woman's hair changed from lengthy and flowing to a braid encircling her head. A bonnet hung from its ties off the back of her head. They took several steps toward the musicians and vaporized. Gone! They just disappeared.

Sheila grabbed Ed's hand and hurried across the street. She stood at the window, gazing in. The musicians continued to play, not noticing her and Ed standing outside. The other couple was gone, nowhere to be seen.

Sheila headed toward the door. Just as she stretched out her hand, reaching for the doorknob, a police officer stepped up behind her.

"I wouldn't do that, Missy. Sir, you should take your little lady back to wherever you came from. This place is closed."

"But officer, the lights are switched on and we watched a couple enter through this doorway before they disappeared," said Ed.

"You must be mistaken. Now move along. We don't want any trouble tonight."

Ed shrugged and took Sheila's hand, directing her back to the hotel. It didn't feel right, but neither said a word. They entered the foyer and went directly up the stairs. The door squealed when they opened it, just as it had before. They closed the door, stared at each other, then embraced one another.

"What was that all about?" said Sheila.

"I don't know. But the officer was intent on moving us away from the store. And obviously, we won't be leaving this room without being heard."

They switched off the lights in their room, pulled two chairs in front of the window and sat watching the storefront for hours.

They marveled at the number of times they saw someone enter the building; watched the clothing transformation; and then they vanished. With each disappearance, they'd ask the other if they witnessed the same occurrence, then discuss the details of what they observed. Neither of them could explain what they saw. It was extremely late when they retired to bed after determining to speak with the hotel management about these events in the morning. They climbed into bed, pulled up the covers, and immediately fell asleep.

They slept later than planned in the morning. Hurriedly, they dressed and went down for breakfast. Clouds were thick, and the winds were picking up. Everyone spoke of an impending storm. After the dining room cleared, Ed and Sheila approached the concierge's desk and explained last night's events.

The concierge looked very serious and shook his head. "I'm sorry, but that just isn't possible. The shop has been shuttered for years. The city struggles to hire someone to do the biannual cleaning in there. And Officer Jentzen, he's one of the easiest going guys around. He wouldn't have chased you off like that. Maybe your wine was stronger than you thought. Sorry I can't be more help. I hope you enjoy your day."

Sheila and Ed glanced at each other, thanked the concierge, held hands, and walked out onto the street.

"Now what?" said Sheila.

"I don't know, but he wasn't even friendly. It was the weirdest exchange I've had with someone in years."

They walked across the street, stopped and stared into the shop windows for a lengthy time.

An elderly woman using a walker approached them. Smiling, she said, "Mighty unique shop, isn't it?"

"Yes," said Sheila. "Can you tell us anything about this building?"

The old woman furtively glanced around the town, turned back to Ed and Sheila, lowered her voice and invited them to her house for afternoon tea.

"I'd like the opportunity to chat with some young folks. We don't have many of them in town anymore."

She provided them with her address. As she turned to leave, she said, "I'll see you at 3."

Sheila and Ed walked the streets in town. Dust devils swirled down the streets as the storm clouds continued to build. Thunder claps rolled in the distance. They entered the local cafe just as the first large drops pelted the sidewalk. Thrilled they could avoid the rain, they slid into a booth and requested to see a menu. After ordering a light snack and a drink, they chatted about the elderly woman they'd met on the street.

"Are we crazy, planning to go to her house for afternoon tea? Do you think she'll be able to explain to us what's happening in this town?" asked Sheila.

Ed said, "She seemed stable enough, though I find it unusual the way she glanced around before talking with us. She was checking for something, but what?"

"Hard to say. But she's the sole person who seemed to validate anything unusual happens in the building. Don't you find that curious?"

"I suspect this may be more exciting than exploring the old mine site," said Ed.

"Oh. If my choices are, go to tea or to the abandoned mine site, we're definitely going to tea."

They both howled with laughter.

The server walked up with their food, set the treats on the table and quickly said, "Let me know if you need anything else." Then she hastened away.

"See, even she thinks we might be a little odd," said Sheila.

"That's okay. I enjoy being a little crazy with you."

The storm passed as quickly as it had arrived. Ed and Sheila began the trek to the old lady's house. The house was perched on a high vantage point, providing full display of the town below and the mine on an adjoining slope. After climbing the steps to the front porch, they tentatively knocked on the door. Shortly, the sound of shoes clicking on the floor became louder, and the door slowly opened. Gleaming hardwood floors and the faint smell of something in the oven greeted them. The little lady they had met on the street stood just inside the door.

"Come in. The kettle's on for tea. It'll be ready in a moment. Please make yourself comfortable in the parlor."

Sheila said, "Thank you."

She and Ed glanced at each other and stepped into the parlor. It was like stepping back in time. The furniture was Victorian in style, all the legs were curved, some with carvings; floral upholstery; and lace doilies on everything. Lace curtains lightly danced on the breeze blowing in from the slightly opened windows. A hand-painted hurricane lamp stood at attention, its post being the front window. Ed and Sheila sat stiffly on the sofa.

The little lady wheeled in a tea cart with plates and unexpected delicacies. She settled in an armchair across from the sofa, with the tea cart beside her. As she poured, she introduced herself.

"I'm sorry, I'm afraid I failed to introduce myself on the street this morning. I'm Mrs. Geller, and I'm so pleased to have you join me for tea. It's been a long time since I've had company."

"Pleased to meet you. We're the Slingers. I'm Ed and this is my wife, Sheila. We're from the front range, here for the weekend. Thank you for the invitation to tea. You're the first person to talk with us and you suggested the shop we were standing in front of was unique, yet you appeared cautious to speak with us on the street. Almost fearful of being seen."

"Oh, heavens no, not fearful. You say you're visiting from the front range, just for the weekend?"

"Yes," said Ed.

"Well, folks in this town disapprove when I tell the truth about the shop. They say it scares off the tourists. I guess I get by with doing so because our family is one of the oldest in town. My relatives started the mine here. There's a lot of history in this town, but about the music shop, I'd advise you to stay away from there. Anyone who has entered the doorway hasn't returned the same person they were. They seem to forget who they were before entering. In fact, they find they cannot leave town once they pass through the doorway of the shop."

"But we saw people walk through the doorway and then they appeared to vanish. How can that be? What happens to them?"

"Ah, yes. People pass through the doorway. The musicians summon people to enter with their siren song. They never return the same. The shop serves as a portal to the past, which leads to your assessment of those who entered suddenly vanishing. They do, kind of. They travel back in time to walk the original streets of Raging River; to try their hand at prospecting, or perhaps lose their life in the trying; to witness gun fights, or be taken away by law marshals. No matter what they experience, when they come back, they have forgotten everything about their prior life and have no desire to leave Raging River. They stay, mostly inhabiting the old homestead area of town, meandering the streets of town by day, only to return nightly to the music shop. If you have family, or like your life on the front range, keep your distance from the shop. My guess is when you checked into the hotel, you listed a next of kin contact information and that's why Officer Jentzen tried to shoo you away."

Sheila gasped, and her voice quivered. "Why do you stay here?"

"I was born here and raised my family here. Like I said, my family started the mine here. This house has been in the family for years. Guess you could say, this town is in my blood. My comfort is in my memories of how the town was when my kids were young. They still return to visit and escape their hectic lives in the city, and mostly to make sure I'm still well. My daughter tries to coax me into moving in with her, and my son reminds me it will not always be safe here. I'm aware, as long as I stay away from the shop, I'm fine. And I struggle with the thought of selling the family home. I doubt either of my kids will want it, so I plan to stay here as long as I'm able. Now, I don't get visitors often, so please tell me about your lives," said Mrs. Geller.

Sheila and Ed spent several hours enjoying the hospitality Mrs. Geller offered. Before leaving, she again cautioned them to stay away from the shop, but invited them to visit her again should they ever return to Raging River. She also warned them that no one in town would substantiate her story, but she provided her children's contact information if they wanted to confirm what she said after they returned to the front range. In fact, she thought Sheila and Ed and her children would get on nicely. They thanked her for her kindness and nonchalantly walked down the hill back to main street and the hotel. Upon their return, the doorman and the desk clerk greeted them. Both were curious about their day's activities and besieged them with questions. Ed was polite, but noncommittal in his responses and Sheila begged off as being tired and requiring rest before dinner. Once in their room, they discussed how curious the staff had acted; how unusual their day and been; and how they found the information unnerving. They committed to contacting Mrs. Geller's children and determined they should discuss none of this further while in town.

After resting, they changed and went down for dinner, only ordering appetizers, wine and dessert. They weren't hungry as their day had been full of food. After a fitful night, they decided to eat breakfast in a different town. They checked out of the hotel early, eager to return to civilization.

Pandemic Limerick

Fall 2020

When is the day
where everyone will say
the world is again open
kids can stop mopin'
at night in bed they will lay

Ornament

The crisp, cold air chilled Samantha's cheeks as she walked the streets Friday evening. The shop windows decorated and lit for the holidays lifted her spirits. Shop doors were open and the fragrances of pine and cinnamon hung in the air. Music drifted into the streets. The atmosphere reminded her of earlier Christmas times and made her happy.` Jake had walked out this morning saying that their relationship was over. He no longer wanted to stay with her. After sobbing throughout the day, she washed her face, dressed and went to the art festival in town. Samantha casually took all this in, feeling like she was a thousand miles away. Suddenly, in a store window she saw this small glass globe, midnight blue, hosting a starlit sky above a stately fir tree decked with fresh snow. The image looked so serene—Samantha immediately entered the store and inquired about the ornament in the window.

"Oh, the ornament is a new piece by Stella," said the clerk.

Samantha immediately recognized the name Stella and realized it would be expensive, yet she knew she needed this ornament. She desired the peace she felt when she looked at it. She dug out her charge card and said, "I'll take it."

"This is lovely, for yourself or a gift for someone else?" said the clerk.

"This is actually a gift for me."

"Well, this is one special gift. I'm sure you'll enjoy it for years to come."

Samantha's excitement grew as she watched the clerk wrap the ornament in multiple sheets of colored tissue paper, place it in a white box filled with soft packing material and tie the box with dark blue ribbon and place it in a bag with the store's logo and name imprinted on the front.

She handed the bag to Samantha, smiled, and said, "Happy Christmas. Enjoy your gift. Stella's art brings pleasure for life."

"Thanks. Happy holidays to you as well."

Samantha recognized a bounce in her step and felt lighthearted as she stepped back into the cold winter air. She stopped by the market to select fresh produce and some cheese before heading back home. Once there she cleared off the mantle and hung the ornament from its accompanying stand. The ceiling spotlight highlighted the piece of art. Samantha smiled each time she looked at it. As she walked through the house, she found things Jake left behind. At first, this made her sad, then frustrated. She didn't want his things underfoot She found a box, then another, and tossed his stuff into them before moving them to the garage. The anger she felt when confronted with Jake's possessions dissipated. As she saw the house becoming void of his things; she felt a calmness settle over her.

This peacefulness lasted through the Christmas holiday season and into the new year. One evening, Samantha's phone rang. Not recognizing the number, she accepted the call.

"Hi Babe."

Samantha was silent.

After a prolonged pause, the caller continued, "Come on. Don't play games. You know this is me, Jake. I'd like to come over and chat with you."

"I don't think we have much to talk about anymore."

"Sammy. Don't be like this."

"Be like what? You left, remember?"

"Okay, okay. How about I stop to pick up the belongings I left at the house, and later we talk a bit? I really need some of those things."

"Saturday morning, 9:30. Be here by 10, or I'll put your boxes on the curb."

Click! Samantha was breathing hard, and her heart was pounding, but she did it. She hung up on Jake.

It was difficult to stay focused at work, and the tension continued to build as the days passed. Samantha was nervous Jake was coming to her house. She wanted his stuff gone, but after moving it to the garage, she'd forgotten about it. She contacted a friend and asked her to stop by the house at 10:15 on Saturday. Additionally, she instructed her friend to be prepared to call the legal authorities if anything appeared abnormal.

Saturday arrived. The house was picked up and fresh. Samantha had showered, pulled her hair back into a ponytail, and dressed in blue jeans and a plaid flannel shirt. The doorbell rang. Her heart raced. She stopped, counted to ten and took several slow, deep breaths before she opened the door. There stood Jake with a bunch of wildflowers.

He stammered. "I, I… bought these for you. Sort of to apologize for interrupting your Saturday."

"Thanks. Come in. You know where the living room is. I'll join you there after I put these in a vase," said Samantha. She turned and headed to the kitchen.

Jake stood in front of the mantle, staring at the ornament by Stella.

"So, Samantha, I was thinking we could give it another try. How about I move back in instead of picking up my stuff?"

Samantha said, "No, I don't think that's a good idea."

"Why? You got someone else living here?"

"That would not be your concern."

"Look, I was stupid. You don't expect me to grovel, do you?"

"No, I don't. I just want you to take your stuff and leave. I have it all boxed and it's in the garage."

"My stuff is in the garage? You already moved me out?"

"You are the one who left. After you took off, I thought I'd make it easier for you and cleaned out your belongings. I wanted to make some space."

"What? Space for junk like that stupid Christmas ornament over there? You left that out after Christmas passed. How much money did you waste on that piece of bric-à-brac?"

"Jake, like I said—please leave. Your boxes are in the garage."

"What about the junk on the mantel?"

"It's not...."

Just then, the doorbell rang. Samantha opened the door. Kristen was on the front porch. She appeared surprised to see Jake in the living room.

"Am I interrupting anything?" said Kristen.

"Darn right you are," said Jake.

"No. No, you're not. Please come in. Jake was just leaving, weren't you Jake?" said Samantha.

Jake shook his head and sighed. "I'll just go through the garage and take my stuff. I know the way out."

Samantha stopped talking and laughed. She looked at Jane, her granddaughter, and handed her the ornament.

"I'll get a box so we can wrap this up for you. You're heading off to college and I want you to have this piece of Stella's art and to remember my story. You're a beautiful, smart young woman. There will be plenty of young fellows who wish to take advantage of you. They will try to convince you, you need them much more than you do. When you look at this art, I want you to remember you are a beautiful, smart woman. You can accomplish anything you set your mind to. You must have confidence in yourself and be willing to strive for your goals. Don't let anyone steal that truth from you.

"Oh, grandma! I love you."

Forgotten

Woman or viper
Passive or aggressive
Both or neither

Participates in carefree outdoor adventures
Yet feels inadequate to others

Maintains a secure job with the school district
Yet finds the work highly stressful

Can be friendly and pleasant
When things are going her way or she wants something

When perceived threats to her lifestyle arise
She becomes aggressive

Forked tongue
Talks one way
Texts another

Says she wants a man in her life
perchance just a man in her bed

Perhaps insecure lonely and afraid
Interactions are difficult
I don't like games

Regrets are few and seldom occupy my thoughts
The last month has been different and the list is growing
Sorry I failed to check references from her last couple
landlords
Sorry I let her into my home
Sorry I modified the lease to accommodate her
Sorry I was upfront about our intention
Sorry I gave her the impression she might be part of the
process
Sorry I keep trying to give her the benefit of the doubt

Challenged to live honorably towards one in your own
home who is so disrespectful

Not sorry, when I leave she will become a forgotten part
of this history
The stressors she's created will pale in comparison
To the great memories I have of this time in my life

Peace is found in knowing she will be forgotten to me

Normal People

Sharon considered herself a normal girl. Well, really a normal woman. She realized she aged out past the "girl" stage some time back. As she contemplated her life, she struggled to understand why she hadn't found "Mr. Right" yet; why she assumed her job was unsatisfying and why everyone else appeared to be healthier and more active than she was. She took part in several out-door activities, riding her bicycle every day, and weather permitting was out on the river daily as well. All of this activity, yet she maintained a full-time job with the school district. She detested all the paperwork and record keeping that went with the job, but appreciated the income it generated. COVID hit, and added a dimension to her job she loathed even more. Working with students on-line didn't provide her with the personal interaction she needed to evaluate their actual progress, but she didn't want the contact risks associated with seeing them face-to-face. Her schedule offered more flexibility with the students not in school. More time to pursue finding Mr. Right.

She'd found a magnificent apartment at a below market rate for the location. She'd finagled the owners to modify the lease at two different times to accommodate her wishes. The view was beautiful; the recently refurbished apartment contained more than she'd dreamed for; and she didn't have to share it with anyone else.

She ensured she paid the rent early every month as she didn't want any reason to lose this apartment. She met a male friend who lived in the neighborhood and enjoyed many outdoor activities. He treated her well, and introduced her to paddle boarding. All looked like it was going well, until he insisted upon maintaining an open relationship and keeping a live-in girl-friend, besides her. This didn't feel good and left Sharon frustrated and often in tears. Then the homeowners had the audacity to list their house for sale. Having lived in the area for some time, Sharon didn't expect this would affect her. It was common for homes to remain on the market for over a year. To her surprise, people flocked to the house in hoards when it first hit the market. Then the owners suggested a lease modification so they, or the new owners, could change her termination date upon a 60 day notice. *How dare they consider asking her to accommodate them? How dare they threaten her comfort and current way of life? How dare they?* These thoughts and words screamed through her mind, occupying most of her waking thoughts. *And how dare Mr. Right not be available to support me? Who's going to help me?*

This began the stage for Sharon of arching her back and attacking like a rabid cat. The venom emitted from her was toxic to all in her vicinity. She'd catch herself, stop, put a smile on her face and change the tone of her voice to sound like a sweet purring kitten.

It was hard on Sharon to maintain the sweet demeanor when feeling so threatened. She felt that any normal person would react the way she was. What she failed to realize was how others could see the rapid switch between pleasant person and rabid animal.

Unbeknownst to Sharon, the owners dug in their bag of tricks and found a small clear mat and placed it in the driveway near her parking spot. They were determined to watch for her to come home at night. They must depress the button at the exact moment Sharon stepped on the mat to successfully execute their plan. They waited and watched.

More people came to the house for inspections. Totally unaware, Sharon grew cocky and fought any of the requests the owners made as they tried to prepare for transferring ownership of the house. Sharon determined if she kept bringing up the lease and her legal rights, they would accommodate any wish she could come up with.

Her next move was defiant. She would not let them take any furnishings out of the apartment, even if they were planning on replacing them, unless the replacement items satisfied her. The lease was hers. It was legal and binding. The place was hers until 31 May.

By day they continued to plan for the transition and by night they would wait and watch.

Then it happened. Sharon had been out with Mr. Right, returning home late at night. It was dark. The owners were watching for her return, and just as she stepped on the clear mat, they pushed the button. At first, Sharon couldn't recognize what was happening. She'd been drinking and considered perhaps she'd had more than she thought. But how could it be? She felt light-headed and like her feet were off the ground. In fact, her body felt like it was rotating and going upward. She started screaming, and the rotating sped up as she continued to escalate into the night sky. She kept spinning and climbing into the night sky as her screams grew fainter and fainter, until she vanished into the dark of the night, spinning into a black hole. Her last thoughts were, *this doesn't happen to normal people.*

The owners stood at their window, watching her disappear out of sight. They heard her diminishing screams. As she vanished from sight, they wiped their hands, gazed into each other's eyes, and smiled.

"We haven't needed to get rid of someone this way in a while. Too bad, she appeared so normal at first."

Remaking

Pause
Projects
We are at home
Like many of you really at home
Perhaps for the first time in ages
At our house this has meant projects
House projects for my hubby
Mostly writing for me
This last week
I took on a project to remake an old family dresser
The chest is sturdy
produced from an era when all wood furniture was
dark
Dark has become so foreboding
It was time for a change
I had a plan
however when I started sanding the finish from the old
piece of furniture
the wood spoke something different to me
Plan abandoned
I kept on working
As I was doing the finish coat
I found my mind wandering to memories of my father
He loved wood and was the one who introduced me to
the beauty of creating with wood.

With intense supervision
he would allow me to work with him on projects in the
basement
Those thoughts brought a smile to mind
For those who know me
I seldom speak of my dad
My memories aren't very pleasant
I've been learning how to remake memories
Instead of replaying the same sad stories
stop the thoughts and replace them with more pleasant
memories
I've been working on this memory project for a few
years
It doesn't change any realities
but it changes what my first thoughts are
when thinking about my father
This weekend wrapped up a remaking project
and contributed to an ongoing remaking project
It's never too late to work on remaking

Grizzly Creek Fire

September 1, 2020, was my first trip through the Glenwood Canyon since the Grizzly Creek Fire. The fire broke out on August 10 and shuttered the main east/west route through Colorado for 13 days. The day we drove through the canyon, the fire was still burning, but the roadways were open. Blackened smoke rolled upward into the sky. In Colorado, the canyon has been one of my favorite places. The terrain is rugged, steep and the canyon walls are close with the river flowing through at the bottom. The interstate and train tracks are on opposite sides of the river.

I marvel at the engineering feat of putting a four-lane interstate highway through such a narrow passageway. There are spans of the highway where one direction of traffic cantilevers over the opposing direction of traffic, all while hugging the canyon walls. There are several tunnels on this section of the thoroughfare; the stories told of their construction speak of man's ingenuity. It's not uncommon for traffic to be shut down because of an accident or a rock slide. The grandeur of the rock walls scream out, expressing the magnitude of God. The ruggedness often leaves me pondering the fortitude and determination of early settlers. How man navigated such terrain is beyond comprehension.

The fire did not devastate the entire canyon. There are many areas that look as I've always seen them. Yet witnessing the blackened tree trunks still standing, the char colored rock walls and the barren rocky ground took my wandering mind to other thoughts.

I, like so many others, enjoy the rugged, natural terrain. Many times I've witnessed big horned mountain sheep scampering up the steep walls. Yes, evidence exists man has been here. The highway itself supports this; then there are the power poles, the barriers to protect the roadway from rock slides and the power plant which harnesses the water from the Colorado River to generate electricity. Man has built homes or ranches encroaching the river or canyon, on land not owned by the Federal Government. This desire to live remotely is shared with many other places in the country.

In years past, lightning would strike and fire would sweep through the canyon, providing a natural cleansing for the land. Underbrush would quickly ignite and it would eradicate diseased trees. Scientists say those fires weren't as large or as deadly as what we experience today because nature managed the growth of the fuel. We've gone to extremes to prevent fires and limit controlled burns. The "Smokey the Bear" fire prevention campaigns of my youth reduced forest fires, but failed. Now instead of numerous smaller fires, more often we have huge fires with lots of fuel to burn. Rains and heavy snowfalls are not as prevalent as in years past. All creating conditions to fuel such catastrophes as this fire. Nature will heal this canyon. For years, the charred tree trunks will reach toward the heavens, marking this event.

Certain Uncertainties

The ground is shifting beneath my feet
My calendar marks the passing of time
Changes in weather confirm this passage
Details require my attention
My mind wanders

Change is happening
One foot planted here and the other
not yet settled in an unknown location
In this straddled state, I feel unbalanced
and perceive time stopped
Not possible! Not true!

I saw you today
You became family
Geography will physically separate us
My heart was saddened

Public message to say good bye
To share how God calls and why we respond
Can I look in your eyes and keep the tears from my own
While living here I've changed
It's no mistake I was here
I will follow the voice that calls
For me to do anything less is unworthy of His calling

The faith we share has bound our hearts together
Location and time cannot undo this bond

Linda L Flynn

We are part of one another's journey
When we meet again
We'll share the stories of life

Live well, my friends
To this you've been called

Does Anyone Have Her Number

Does anyone have her number? This was the question everyone was asking. To an onlooker, elegantly dressed men and women filled the hall. Nothing appeared out of place. Tall floral arrangements graced the tables, many located in front of large mirrors. The floors gleamed. The long hallway sported several pairs of double-doors, all of which remained closed. A soft buzz filled the space as the guests lingered in the hallway, champagne glasses in hand.

Charlotte agreed to host the dinner party, the culminating annual event for this group. She had the skills and grace to make anyone feel comfortable, resulting in them being able to recognize being treated special; they all loved it! Charlotte spent weeks planning the evening. Barlow, a national celebrity, renown for her sharp eye as an art critic, was in the country. Charlotte invited her to the event and asked if she would moderate a contest the local group had sponsored for the evening.

The painting group was ecstatic when they learned Barlow would be the moderator of their art contest at the dinner event. Now, on this evening, one could feel the excitement surge in the hallway as they waited for the guest of honor. The doorbell rang, and a hush fell over the crowd. The butler returned and said, "Madame Barlow has arrived with Miss Christine."

Charlotte rushed over to greet Madame Barlow. Many people gathered in small huddles. The sound of soft whispers filled the room. Miss Christine was voluptuous, with beautiful ivory colored skin. She was wrapped in a silver fox coat, she refused to surrender to the butler. She hung close to Madame Barlow's side, making it difficult for Charlotte to greet Madame Barlow.

Finally, Charlotte got everyone's attention, introduced the guest of honor, and Miss Christine and announce it was time to enter the dining hall.

Madame Barlow turned to Charlotte, "Really? We will eat first? I assumed this was an evening for painting and then I'd judge the paintings. I brought Miss Christine along as the subject for the evening. At that moment, almost on cue, Miss Christine let her fox coat slide off her shoulders and drop to the floor. She stood there in a silver threaded negligee and heels, with her back erect and her head held high. She stared into the crowd as they gasped. Never in their wildest fantasies had they envisioned this for the evening. Some men chuckled while the women scowled. Charlotte stuttered.

"I, I, hum, there must have been some misunderstanding."

One could see the defiance cross Barlow's face. "Misunderstanding? What do you mean? I never attend an event without a subject. And I never judge painting not done in my presence. Surely you knew this!"

No one in attendance had seen Charlotte so off balance before. She could carry her own in any conversation, always remained so calm and collected. But this evening, it was obvious Charlotte was embarrassed and uncertain how to proceed.

She paused, and said, "Well, actually, I was unaware of those requirements. I've heard of you and your notoriety only from what I've read in the papers, the art sections, to be more accurate. I thought having you judge our paintings would be the pinnacle event for the year and inspire all of us to continue painting."

"Humph. I've already told you my requirements for judging. I can only imagine this group of dowdies only paint still-life," said Barlow.

She turned to Miss Christine and said, "I think we should leave. I'm sorry if I embarrassed you for bringing you to such a stodgy group of people this evening. Sir, pick up her wrap and fetch our car. I have no intention of staying here any longer."

As Barlow and Miss Christine walked out the door, Charlotte turned to her guests and shrugged.

"I have no words to explain this evening. But the chef has prepared an amazing dinner. You're my friends, and we always have a grand time when we're together. I hope in the future we'll be able to laugh about tonight."

One gentleman cleared his throat. "Here, here. I say we toast Charlotte for saving us from that horrid woman."

Here, Here, resounded throughout the room.

Charlotte tipped her head and smiled at her friends.

"Thank you. Let's go have dinner."

The doors to the dining hall opened. Ohh's and Ahh's filled the air as the guests entered the room. The décor was stunning in its simplicity. Bold primary colors filled the room. Charlotte used basic shapes in as many ways as possible; square plates, round placemats, triangular glassware, and so on.

Everyone found their place at the table. The servers brought out multiple courses. Comments abounded about how delectable everything tasted. Then the next course arrived, and they were pleasantly surprised again. The main entrée was the delight of the meal. No one could believe Charlotte had flown in buffalo steaks. Flaming flan completed the meal.

After they finished their after-dinner drinks, they agreed to gather in the room where their art was on display.

The group moved throughout the gallery and paused at each piece to discuss the person's work. They decided a contest winner was unnecessary. They were all winners because they pursued something they enjoyed and shared it with others.

Charlotte heard many say this was the best contest event the group ever experienced. She said goodbye to each guest as they departed. As the last guest departed and the door closed, Charlotte leaned back against it. She smiled and then giggled. It was inconceivable to imagine how an evening which began with the snafu caused by Barlow and Miss Christine could turn into a rich gathering of shared friendship.

As she thought about her friends, her heart filled with gratitude for them. Her friends were with her on favorable days and bad days, yet accepted her as she was; despite circumstances, these were people she could share a wonderful time with. Before heading upstairs to her bedroom, she peaked into the dining room and thanked the staff for all their efforts and for making the evening so enjoyable for all.

The In-Between Space

November 2020

House sold
Packed up
Moved out
Furnishings stored
Offer accepted
Details negotiated
Dates set
Time and space between
Where do my feet call home
Contemporary loft apartment
fulfills this in-between state
The hum of city life surrounds me
Music from a nearby establishment fills the night air
Merely two blocks away is the beach
visible from the roof-top balcony
Here my brain processes recent activity
Spinning
Spinning
Thoughts whirl
Decisions made
Arrangements scheduled
Brain stopped swirling
Against the blue sky
Palm trees sway
The ocean calls
Walks on the beach

Linda L Flynn

Marine layer rolls in
enveloping all in mist
Tension releases
Comfort comes as the time to relocate draws near

Tears and Joy

Fall 2020

I am so captivated by my new home
yet often find myself close to tears.
Why?
I reach for the phone.
Then not.
She's gone, no longer in this world.
I now recognize…
She was the one person
who appreciated my need to travel and explore;
Acknowledging, she had roots, but I had wings.
Vicariously
she traveled and explored through my eyes.
I wove words
creating intricate images of places and things.
Her excitement in these tales was indisputable.
I found joy in sharing
sights
events and
adventures
then recognized her enjoyment.
There was no boasting or bragging
only sharing
as such
it was received.

Now I find myself with no-one
to share these experiences with.
She would have been overwhelmed
by the variety of plants surrounding me.
Even I'm astonished and captivated
by the vegetation and the prospect of assorted fruit.
Tears and joy mingle
knowing some things are passed on
genetically without knowledge;
All is as it should be
such is life.

My interest in plants
needed different soil and climate for birth.
That part of her lives on in me.
Sweet tears
drop to the ground
as I work the soil.

Common Things

Days of unpacking
Handling dishes
Glass-wear and the like
Stirred memories of days long gone

Stories told
History shared
To some it's just a bowl
I know my sister owns its mate
As my grandmother and her friend each owned one
Then there sits the cake plate which was my great-grandmother's
Passed from one generation to the next
Just as the love of dishes and glassware was passed
Stories shared as we handled these dining pieces

Tears wait barely below the surface
Because these conversations live only in my memories
Missing the shared chatter and laughter
I know this is far better for her
Surrounded by these items causes thoughts to flood my mind like a torrent
As the dish-ware finds home in cupboards
My mind and spirit settle

In future days I will take a piece out to use here or there

Memories will be resurrected
I expect the thoughts to then be more gentle
This is a point in time I'm grateful for the bounty of
remembrances
And wait for gentle days

People Say

… the mountain casts a spell over folks who live near it. When one leaves the area, the spell causes that person to never really leave, but at least continue to return.

Maybe…

Maybe not…

We left the area about six weeks ago, then returned to retrieve a vehicle we'd left behind. Our conversations revealed we each felt happy to be back in town, driving the streets, seeing a few friends, enjoying the sights and having food from several favorite places.

Let there be no mistake. We know our new home, the region where we live, the town we're part of is exactly where we are supposed to be and we're thrilled to begin this new adventure in our life journey.

We've returned to locations of previous homes to visit friends, but never experienced the feeling of simple happiness by just being in the area. Perhaps there is a spell on us from the mountain, or maybe it's because we each experienced so much personal growth and deepened our spiritual lives here; made many friendships and memories. We changed while living here. We're not the same people we were when we moved here. We smile, knowing we'll be back again.

Have you ever felt like living somewhere changed who you are?

Geography

You say you want to trade in salt and a snow shovel for a pail and a sand shovel.

....and I think of the winter night's sky. The color of blue is like no other-and the stars are so numerous and clear; sparkling like little diamonds against the dark blue velvet.

....jump to another scene and I see one of the Grand Tetons reflected in Jenny Lake. Picturesque and majestic.

....jet set to the top of a rocky cliff overlooking the Northern Atlantic watching wild waves crashing against the rocky shoreline.

And so it goes. With all these glorious places, how does one choose?

....and actually, what choice do we have but to find God's glory in each of them?

My Life—2020

The clocked chimed midnight. I gazed around the table; we appeared to be just normal people enjoying an annual tradition. Others might say our relationship is friendly, loosely held together by our annual get-together. Each of us meeting for the evening would express something different.

New Year's Eve is the night we gather for our annual tradition—a four course Fondue dinner, each couple contributing to the food, the preparation and the clean-up; a recounting of the year; dreams and expectations for the coming year; laughter; and way too much food. I count New Year's Eve as my favorite holiday because of the depth of relationship with these friends, and how our lives have become interwoven. In retrospect, I recognize each of the households represented performs outreach, which goes deep into the community. The youngest among us has returned to college for a second career so he can work as a counselor, helping those with mental health issues. This special valley, dubbed by me many years ago as the "happy valley," has many who suffer from depression and a suicide rate above national averages. Another household has one who works as a school counselor further down the valley where many who are less fortunate and often forgotten live. Another represented family is home to the regional director of "Operation Christmas Child." This is her passion, and she glows when talking about it. We go to Ireland to help the local pastors in County Kerry with whatever they request from us. Our lives focus on contributing to society, and this night, we share the joys of our work with one another. We all shared our perceived expectations for 2020.

Even that night, I experienced a momentary twinge, suggesting maybe I didn't belong in this geographical location anymore. This thought flashed through my mind periodically since the summer of 2019. I pushed it away whenever it came to mind, just as I did on New Year's Eve; I chose not to consider this possibility. We ended the evening. I celebrated another year of life and we returned to Ireland for four weeks. While there, we reconnected with those we'd met during our stay in 2019. Relationships renewed and friendships deepened. We returned to the US early February 2020, just as travelers found themselves questioned about being in China within the last two weeks.

Soon after arriving home, Europe responded decisively in an effort to contain or control the spread of COVID-19 and its potential effect upon their people. In the United States, there was no consistent message. Some people were sure it wouldn't affect us here; others were fearful this could be a precursor to end times; it conflicted other individuals about what was believable as messaging was contradictory and misleading. Leadership provided no cohesive message for the country. Various individual states attempted to provide guidance found lacking at a national level. They discovered some of their population was thankful for the direction, and it agitated others. The government left many Americans to traverse COVID-19 on their own, or join ranks with one of the conflicting political sides. I still find this shocking and embarrassing.

On a personal level, I lived in Colorado, a place where the governor imposed guidelines trying to contain the virus, so my husband and I voluntarily eliminated going out in social situations. I found this easier than my hubby. We worked on projects at our home, and I spent more time writing, more time working on creative efforts, more time cooking new dishes.

I found companionship in writing groups. The group I connect with in Ireland converted to Zoom and invited me to join with them. The local group in Colorado went from meeting monthly to meeting weekly via Zoom. Other groups sprang up using Facebook and various social media platforms. I found I established better writing disciplines, which allowed me to give voice to feelings and frustrations about this unusual time and camaraderie among others who put words to paper. Relationships with other writers have been a source of comfort, strength and encouragement during the surprises of 2020.

July found us traveling to California where we socially distanced there just as we had at home while staying at the residence of a family member. We attended an out-door wedding of less than 12 people. The change of location and scenery filled a need I was unaware I had. We both returned to Colorado refreshed and relaxed.

My mom, who'd been living in a care facility and plagued with Alzheimer, fell. The pandemic had added more changes to her already altered life. Her partner of 49 years could no longer visit her daily, creating a deterioration in quality of life for both of them. After her fall, as her health continued to decline, my step-dad was allowed to spend time with her. I'm thankful he was there. They held hands. She fell asleep and left this world. I am grateful it worked out this way after her fall, yet that doesn't diminish the sadness associated with losing my mom.

We continued to remain socially isolated, going out for necessities and the outdoor church services. One day while we were waiting to hear the schedule for mom's memorial service, we each admitted having a sense we should reside in Southern California. It seemed unusual. We both enjoyed living in Colorado, where we're involved in the community and the church, and loved our home. Yet the feelings persisted. We started sorting things out at the house; got packing materials; listed our house for sale; traveled to the mid-west for my mom's memorial service. Within a few short days of returning home, our house was under contract.

In 2020, when many times it seems the world put the brakes on living, our lives continued to spin with activities, paperwork, legalities, planning and decisions. Soon after we signed a contract for the sale of the Colorado home, we had another house under contract to purchase in California. Similar activities that had us reeling in Colorado were now under way in California. There were days when I felt stretched thin, being pulled in two different geographic locations.

Everything came together in Colorado; we moved our belongings and put them into storage in California. We moved into a furnished loft apartment with small suitcases. A pleasant apartment, yet in some ways, I felt I was in storage, waiting to move into our new home. The list of activities, decisions, legalities and paperwork created an atmosphere as dizzy as the one in Colorado, with a process much different from anywhere else we had lived. Some days we laughed at this and said it was a learning curve, other days we shook our heads not understanding and then there were days we just couldn't think anymore. Through it all, the process kept moving forward and the day to taking possession kept moving closer. I knew I would soon break out of storage.

COVID-19 outbreaks surged to new heights. Again, the only leadership occurred at state levels. The 2020 presidential elections gobbled up much of the broadcast time and considerable brain space for many individuals. I find the all-consuming efforts required to move have allowed me to disengage from the partisan conversations. I've checked the news a few times per week using various on-line sources. The divides in the nation regarding values and ideals have grown wider. Am I part of a process that appears to be a failing experiment and question, will democracy survive? I turn my attentions to making a move, trying to stay healthy, to support and encourage those I love and watch for the outcome to become clear.

As the close of 2020 draws near, I settle into a new house. My thoughts return to that New Year's Eve night, to the conversation, laughter, and fellowship we shared. Such fine memories! That evening, we discussed how unfathomable it seemed to even say 2020. Is *now* a sign of the future or an anomaly designed to awaken us from our slumber and cause us to consider matters more important than ourselves?

Ode to 2020

Some people say

2020 was the lost year

I disagree

2020 was the year
I became focused
I got serious about my writing
Enjoyed contact with writers from around the world
Was challenged and encouraged
To be bold
To let the words out
To trust my voice
Learned the peace of spending time with my thoughts
Found joy in simple pleasures
Around my house
With my husband
Enjoyed time to read
And then read some more
Cooked some amazing meals
Wrote and wrote and then wrote some more
Became comfortable with Zoom and its limitations
Met other creatives who shared their struggles during
this time

Up rooted myself
Moved
Settled in to find myself surrounded by unknown
plants
Doors opened to new learning
Writing continues
Meeting neighbors and others
Continue Zoom meetings with writers
Projects progressing
2020 was the year

New Home Memories in the Making

COVID-19 finds me basically locked down in my new home. I comply with the governor's request to stay home by choice. This home, new to me, leaves much to explore and discover. We have 2 plus acres of hillside land covered with citrus and other fruit trees, fir trees, nut trees, deciduous trees, numerous cacti and succulents, which I know nothing about. We found the land neglected and overgrown. This reality, coupled with our lack of knowledge about the plants, generates both interest and frustration. I'm excited to know our property grows multiple varieties of oranges, lemons, limes, loquat, apricots, apples, peaches, almonds, dragon fruit, several types of berries and who knows what else? Water is expensive and the irrigation system needs work. They lined the patio with plants, but with no actual design plan.

Most boxes are unpacked, meaning most objects have discovered their space in this home. We're still waiting for the dining room furniture and bookcases. Those pieces will arrive sometime between mid-January and June. Once those items arrive, I'll feel more settled.

The house is a Spanish-style home with wide verandas around three sides of the house. The building, upon further examination, reveals a box type structure. Those covered decks with their arched openings and soft lighting create a welcoming atmosphere as you approach the property. The interior of the home continues the square design throughout, resulting in a floor plan that accommodates our lifestyle. Gone are the soaring ceilings from the previous house, replaced instead with a multitude of windows in each room, allowing soft light to enter throughout the day. The rooms seem to flow effortlessly from one to the other, making it easy to move from one space to another.

While waiting to finish the interior, we've turned our attention outward to the land. First the patio, as we see ourselves using this area often. It fills a need to expand living into outdoor spaces. We've tackled the potted plants, arranging like varieties together, creating a bigger visual impact by the groupings. Irrigation is being tweaked to simplify the maintenance and group plantings by their type and water needs. We added additional pots and seeded some with produce we hope to grow here. Several other large pots will become home to Dragon Fruit which were scattered around the property. Many evenings I've scoured the internet for information on how to care for specific plants; their watering needs, how to transplant them; what to expect for growth, blooming, and fruit production. We completed one zone on the property. The first of the winter rains came and with it an abundance of wonderful fragrances so intoxicating, yet I cannot label them. Oh yes, the patio will be used often.

Both hubby and I moved in different directions. He's undertaking the growth on a rock outcropping on the driveway approach to the house and scheming how to move young agave plants from one area to another to create an "agave forest." Me, I'm working on both the potted plants lining the walk to the front door and an outdoors sitting zone on the side of the property where rosemary, lantana, jade, lavender and other unidentified plants have become so overgrown I can't tell where one ends and another begins. Some are species I've struggled to grow elsewhere, so to encounter them here, taller than I, is a bit daunting. I've attacked these plants with my pruning shears and an attitude of what must be done, must be done. Either the plant will thrive, or I must replace it with something else. Snip, snip, snip, and there is space between plants. The ground is visible and I can see over the top of them. I trudge my heap of pruning waste to another pile waiting for Tuesday's green waste pickup. I still can't decide how to correct the front walkway pots and lay awake at night pondering options.

Since moving here, I've accomplished more outside work than I've done in years. At day's end, I'm tired. I long to return to Ireland and friends there. Yet, I understand COVID has shuttered much of the world. Many days I forget about that reality as I labor to make this new abode our home; creating an interior atmosphere pleasing to us and welcoming to friends; working to tame some natural growth so we can maximize the production of citrus available here and share the fruit with others, while I ponder when I'll slow down and get back to my writing.

The day ends with dinner indoors. Afterwards, we settle in the living room surrounded by belongings we've had for years, all placed in unique locations within this new dwelling. This residence is rapidly claiming our hearts and feels much like home. It won't be long before this house sings our song.

A Sunday Afternoon

I never would have thought
I'd be sitting outside under an umbrella
Enjoying a breeze blowing inland from the shore
With no view of the ocean in sight
Watching small lizards darting around the patio

The neighbor's palm trees appear as green tinsel
blowing in the breeze
The long pine needles wave as the wind passes by
Eucalyptus and other tall trees sway hinting of potential
incoming weather
The air is filled with the smell of sweet alyssum
And the sound of various birds fluttering from one
branch to another

I'm content to sit here and soak up the atmosphere
Oblivious to the potted plants begging for attention
Today it's enough to absorb the environment
To be filled with gratitude for being surrounded by
beauty
To allow the peace of the day to wash over my soul

As I enjoy this place called home

Hats

The day arrived when the enormous trunk was delivered to Sara's doorstep. She inherited her great aunt's personal possessions. Other family members had received small tokens, and it shocked Sara, her distant aunt had left her seemingly so much compared to the others. She directed the delivery man to place the trunk in her front hallway. It was a large leather bound traveling trunk, red in color. Red seemed like a rare color for this piece. Days before, she had received the parcel containing the key and a short handwritten note from her Aunt Sara. The writing was spidery and difficult to read. She could determine that Aunt Sara was her namesake, and that Aunt Sara regretted not having a closer relationship with her. She hoped Sara was well and that she might possibly understand something about her namesake from the items within the trunk.

Sara retrieved the key from her desk, inserted it in the lock, and slowly turned the key, listening to the clicking noise as the lock released and popped open. She lifted the lid and stared. The inside of the trunk was lined with black velvet. The box appeared to be filled with hats of various styles. Sara picked a tam from the top of the pile. It was dark green. After twirling it around in her hands, she plopped it on her head, stood up, and headed to the mirror. To her surprise, it made her look perky. Sara never considered herself a "hat girl" even though she enjoyed looking at hats and thought other women looked chique in hats.

She sighed, pondering what she would do with all these hats. Returning to the trunk, she continued to look through the hats and then, beneath them, discovered several small wooden boxes. As she lifted out the boxes, an envelope dropped into the trunk. As Sara retrieved it from the trunk, she recognized the handwriting. It was similar to the note she had received with the key. She sat on the floor against the couch, holding the envelope. Carefully opening the envelope, her mind wandered. *What is the importance of trunk full of hats? Why me? There are many other family members?* Extracting the paper from the envelope, Sara could see there were several pages. She read. Obviously, there was much about Aunt Sara that she didn't know. The family rarely spoke of her. The letter revealed some of those reasons, at least from Aunt Sara's perspective.

The Cleaner and the Hoarder

Christine stopped in her tracks and just looked around. Boxes and piles were everywhere in the hallway. She gingerly stepped over some shoes by the entrance, then peaked around the corner of the next area. Every flat surface held haphazard piles. Someone filled the corners with boxes, books, games, and an assortment of other things. How did I get myself into this she wondered.

So confidently she accepted the job her friend offered. Her business was organizing and cleaning up other people's belonging, originally this job sounded no different from any other. But this time it was her friend she was working for; a friend who wanted to surprise her mom and clean up the house.

Christine was used to the hesitation when she met with a client. She scheduled her work when they would be away from the property. This job was different; mom was out of town for several days. Christine sensed tension as she moved through the house.

Inspiration

When the sky turns dark
I lay my head
onto my pillow
My mind stirs and spins
Great thoughts and ideas
abound

I long for sleep
Yet ponder
story starts
vivid scenes
Words
easily flow
with twists and turns
My weary body
cannot arise

I assure myself
I'll write the words
in the daylight

Slumber overtakes me
Later
I rub my eyes
to the pink glow of morning
as the sun peaks
above the horizon

Linda L Flynn

A new day
with all it offers
Gratitude fills my heart
But alas
Some thief snuck into
my room while
the stars twinkled and shone

My wonderful writing thoughts
have vanished
leaving not a remnant
nor evidence
of who stole
my inspiration

Superstition

Jane jumped out of bed and approached the window. Cautiously, she pulled back the curtain to peer into the night. Some unrecognizable sound screeched through the air. Coyotes howled incessantly and the neighbor's dogs whined and barked. Jane shivered and pulled her shawl around her shoulders. Shadows stretched across the yard as the trees swayed in the wind. She saw dark bodies moving in the street. Bodies with hoods pulled over their heads. One body turned, looking at her house. She let the curtain drop from her hand and stepped back from the window. Her heart pounded loudly, it's sound filled the room. Why hadn't her parents returned yet? Visions from the movie she saw replayed in her head. Horrid things happened on Friday the 13th. Why didn't she stay at her friend's house this evening?

Jane returned to her bed; sitting up with her back against the headboard, she pulled her knees to her chest and wrapped her blankets around herself. With every sound, she jumped, and her heart thumped even louder. She stared at her clock and watched the seconds tick by. When would her parents come home? When would they come home? It was already 10:30. Lightning struck, followed by the sharp clap of thunder. Jane jerked and started shaking.

The sound of screeching tires and a whimpering dog filled her ears. But she found herself frozen and unable to move. The unknown filled her with fear. She clutched her pillow to her face and buried her sobs in the soft cotton fabric. Jane was shaking and crying uncontrollably when her mother walked into the room and over to her bed. She sat on the side of the bed, and Jane screamed.

"Honey, what is wrong?"

"Oh, Mom. I'm so glad you are home. There were a lot of bad things happening tonight. And more were to come."

"Why would you say that?"

"It's Friday the 13th, and…, and…, and coyotes were howling, and dogs were barking and…"

Mom pulled Jane close. "Honey, why don't we go downstairs and make some hot chocolate? Everything's going to be alright."

"Mom! It's Friday the 13th. It will not be alright. Something is going to happen."

"Jane, let's get something to drink. Dad and I are home now. Friday the 13th, is a lot of superstition. We can talk about that downstairs."

One Wild and Precious Life

The writing prompt arrived in my email:

"Tell me, what do you plan to do with your one wild and precious life?" by Mary Oliver

What a crazy thing to think about…

Especially after today, after spending some time with a couple of friends. They each commented, they thought I've lived a very interesting and unusual life. I think about it as my life. Nothing unusual or special, just my life.

Then the prompt arrives. I have to change it some so I can better relate to it.

How am I going to live my one wild and precious life?

Good question.

I guess when I was younger, I was a little wild. I married, had kids, and assumed I had to do what everyone else thought I needed to do. This proved to be difficult, impossible, and, in many ways, boring. Yet somehow, I learned diverse skills, which served me well throughout my life; I made many friends during those years. I moved often, refining the skills needed to adapt to life in different locations. The bottom fell away from my life and the moving parts I was trying to hold together swirled out of my hand as though falling through a black hole.

I perceived I was lost in the dark of night, yet enjoyed a sense of weightlessness finally untethered from all the expectations of others. This was a strange time where I stumbled much.

Sure, there were plenty of folks who thought they could put their expectations on me, but I had learned the important, self-protective, freeing lesson of boundaries.

I arrived on the other border of my dark space freer, with more self-confidence. Ultimately, I became more positive, happier and less fearful.

Life is precious and I now appreciate all it offers. I aim to spend the rest of it making life better for others, or being real to other individuals. I have some wild times in my writing experiences and deeply enjoy the friendships I share with other writers. Perhaps my writing persona is legitimately the wild me.

As writers, we all long to say words others will hear, will want to hang onto, words we'll be remembered for. These writing friendships have helped open creative thoughts I never knew were there. I'll spend the rest of my days putting words to paper.

Writing Valentines

Sara arrived home breathless. Today was the day she and Carol were out shopping for wedding dresses. The girls filled the day with laughter, tasty food, an abundance of dresses and material for many future memories. The girls, best friends since youth, were getting married in three months at a joint celebration ceremony. They considered themselves lucky their respective future husbands had become friends and agreed to the joint event. Both mothers encouraged the girls to have separate events, but to no avail. Sara realized there were some challenges, as each of the girls had different styles. Yet their friendship was strong and they wanted to celebrate together.

Sara threw open the door and said, "Mom, I'm home. I'm home, mom."

"No need to yell. I'm in the laundry. I'll be there in a minute."

Sara threw herself down in the yellow overstuffed chair in the living room. Within seconds, she jumped back up and was pacing in front of the fireplace.

"Come-on mom."

When her mom walked into the room, Sara ran over and threw her arms around her neck.

"Oh mom, you won't believe it. I found the dress of my dreams. It's perfect! I can't wait for you to see it."

"Tell me about it. I'm dying to hear."

Sara began detailing the flowing train, the embroidered lace trim, the princess neckline, and then the phone rang. At first tempted to let it ring, her mother shook her head and said, "One of us should answer that. Your father is due back from his business trip, and I'm expecting his call."

"Oh, alright," said Sara as she ran into the hall to pick up the phone.

"Sara, is that you?" said Carol.

"Yes, I'm just telling mother about the dress. What did your mom say when you got home?"

"Mom was standing there with an envelope for me. She told me the card arrived with this beautiful bunch of yellow roses. The hallway smelled heavenly from the roses. I tore open the envelope and found this beautiful Valentine's Day card. I expected it to be from Stephen cuz he's always so thoughtful, and it is Valentine's Day."

Sara sensed the excitement in Carol's voice building.

"Ok, ok. Carol, do you mind getting to the point? Trent will be here shortly. We're going out for dinner."

"I can't identify who sent it. The card read, 'Carol, you always caught my eye, but I was too shy to approach you. I still think about you; about how you looked; how graceful you were; and how soothing your voice was. I read about your engagement in the paper and was heartbroken. I knew I had to reach out before the fateful day of your wedding. If interested in meeting me for real, I'll be at Jack's Pub on February 16th at 6pm. Devoted...' Well? What do you think?"

"You're giving this any consideration? Are you crazy? You and Stephen are engaged to be married. Why did you say *yes* if you're still considering other men's approaches?"

"Sara, don't you think it sounds intriguing?"

"Carol?!"

"Sara, honestly. You don't think it sounds interesting to have someone from your past, an unknown someone, show up and express interest?"

"We're getting married in less than 90 days. The timing seems suspect to me. Your attitude is concerning to me."

"Sara! Don't say such a thing. You know I love Stephen and I also love a little intrigue."

Sara's mom walked into the hallway and gave her a quizzical look. Sara just shrugged her shoulders, tipped her head and made a face.

Mom mouthed, "Trent will be here soon."

"Carol, gotta run. I want to freshen up my makeup before Trent gets here. Bye."

"Sara, you were so abrupt. What was that all about?"

"Don't have time right now, Mom. We can talk tomorrow." Sara ran upstairs. She wanted to splash her face with cold water, hoping to wash the shock she was experiencing down the drain.

Trent scheduled reservations at a small bistro. They enjoyed an amazing evening of small plates, listened to the jazz music while talking and laughing about their upcoming wedding. They found the bistro crowded and the music loud, so Trent didn't notice the moments Sara drifted off into thought. Sara chose not to mention her phone call with Carol. She hoped Carol would come to her senses and they could return to focusing on their joint wedding.

Before the evening ended, Sara mentioned to Trent she planned to visit her grandparents for the weekend. She wanted to go to the farm. Trent smiled. He expressed it was a splendid plan, and he'd see her when she returned.

After arriving home, she packed her overnight bag, wrote a note telling her parents where she was going, and fell into bed. Instead of sleeping, she tossed and turned much of the night, knowing she had to leave and clear her thoughts. Carol might actually ruin their joint wedding. Eventually, Sara must have fallen asleep as the alarm jerked her awake. She slipped into her clothes, grabbed her bags, and left the note on the table for her parents. The drive to the farm was peaceful; the morning was beautiful. Sara arrived at the farmhouse and surprised her grandparents. It pleased them to see her. The visit was refreshing and cleared her mind.

Her grandparents didn't ask why she was there or seem surprised to see her. They enjoyed her company and showed her around the farm. It was like any other trip to her grandparent's house, and Sara loved her time with them.

Monday morning, Sara kissed her grandparents goodbye. "I'm looking forward to seeing you both at the wedding. Thanks for letting me stop by on the spur of the moment."

"Honey, you're always welcome here. It's your home away from home," said her grandma.

Grandpa said, "Just don't stay away so long next time."

They all laughed as she jumped in her car and drove down the lane and back to town. When she stopped to purchase a coffee, she retrieved her phone from the glove box and checked for messages. She saw Carol had called multiple times, leaving both voice and text messages. Immediately, Sara's thoughts returned to the uncertainty of what Carol might do and how Carol's actions might affect her own wedding. Sara sat there, staring at her phone. *Do I listen to these messages, or just call Carol?* She recognized she needed to know if the wedding plans had changed or not. She didn't want to have this conversation in her mom's presence, or to have her mom remind her they should not have planned a joint ceremony. So she phoned Carol.

Carol answered the call on the first ring. "Hi Sara. Where have you been? I've been trying to get a hold of you. I can't wait to tell you about the weekend. I have so much to tell."

"Stop. Stop right there! I needed a break, so I escaped to the farm. I wanted to clear my mind. There is no need for any more drama in my life. The wedding is my focus. The only information I want to hear is if you're still marrying Stephen and if our joint wedding is moving forward as planned or not."

"Wow, you don't sound like yourself. We've always shared our secrets with one another and right now, you sound distant."

"We've been planning our weddings. My wedding is the most important event in my life—and I don't want it messed up. So, are you and Stephen getting married or not?"

"Of course, silly. Stephen is the best person on the earth for me. I couldn't find a nicer guy. The wedding is on. Be there or be square."

"Good."

"Now, can we talk about my weekend?"

"NO. I don't want to hear about it."

"Are you okay?"

"Yup."

"Doesn't sound like it," said Carol.

"I have to drive back to town and then stop at the office to wrap up my current project. Why don't you stop over tomorrow evening so we can review some wedding arrangements? Okay?"

"Sure, see you then."

"Okay, bye."

Sara disconnected the call and took a deep breath.

Carol stood there holding the phone, wondering what had just happened.

The girls continued their wedding planning. No-one was aware of the growing rift in their relationship. It was different when they were alone. Gone was the easy banter and free flowing conversation. Every time Carol attempted to bring up the February 16th meeting, Sara would shut her down. The wall between the two women continued to grow deeper and higher.

The day of the wedding was glorious. All efforts put into planning the event paid off. It was a day to remember. Before anyone realized what happened, each of the happy couples escaped on their honeymoons.

Sara sighed a sigh of relief, knowing each husband planned a separate get-away, as she was unsure how long she could avoid Carol's confrontation now that the wedding was behind them. *Oh, bother. We're both married now. Surely Carol will drop all this nonsense and focus on being Stephen's wife.*

The two couples often went out together for the evening. It wasn't long before each household grew with the addition of children. Carol and Stephen had a boy and a girl, whereas Sara and Trent had two daughters. Occasionally, when the children were young, and the girls were alone, Carol tried to discuss the past. But Sara was unwilling to entertain the conversations. Then Carol just stopped talking about it. Both families were involved in the many activities of raising kids. In the summer, they would often spend an afternoon together at the pool, or go hiking and pack a picnic. When they were together, it felt like one big family.

Sara was unprepared for the day Trent arrived home from work, distraught. She knew he loved his work and couldn't imagine what would have caused him to be so upset. "Stephen called me this morning to say Carol took off late last night. She left the kids saying she wasn't coming back. She couldn't play charades anymore. He is shook up. Do you know anything about this?"

"No, I haven't seen Carol since the last time we went out. What's he going to do?"

"He's called his parents and they're coming to stay for a while to help with the children and to sort things out. I don't think he knows what he's going to do. Are you aware of any reason Carol would leave like this? Can we do anything to help?"

Sara just shook her head and said, "I can't believe this."

Later in the week, Sara received a letter. She tore it open and read,

"Dear Sara, I'm sure you've heard by now I've left. I can't live without Bill anymore. I've tried to talk with you about my feelings, but you have shut me out. I need to go where I feel loved. The children need little care. Please help Stephen when you can and make sure the kids know their mother loves them dearly. I will always fondly remember the friendship we shared and doubt I will ever have another friend like you. Love, Carol,"

Sara fell into the nearest chair and sobbed. Her heart hurt for Stephen, and for Carol and Stephen's children. She finally stood up from the chair, folded the letter and placed it in her jewelry box, not knowing if she would tell anyone about this or not.

How could she explain to anyone she and Carol had been friends for next to forever, yet she never let Carol tell her about the February 16th meeting? And now, how could she explain her years of silence? No, stashing the letter in her jewelry box and remaining quiet seemed like the wisest action.

Life went on. Sara and Trent remained friends with Stephen. Some times after they had been together, Sara would become withdrawn and angry. When this happened, she would go to the garden and tend her flowers. Her memories took her back to the fateful Valentine's Day when the cracks in her friendship with Carol revealed themselves. It made her angry Carol had put her in this position. It's a position Sara doesn't feel like she can escape from; one where she would be forced to choose between her loyalty to Stephen and Carol as a couple, or just to Carol. As she jerked out weeds, she recognized anger at herself over her own immaturity of being more concerned about her wedding day than the needs of her friend. She had this building frustration nagging at her because she knew the truth, which was her own wedding, was of greater importance than Carol's feelings. Nor was she able to discuss any of this with Trent. Sara realized she wasn't a reliable friend and questioned how to improve on being a better wife. She recognized somehow she had to discuss this with Trent.

She swallowed hard and went inside to call her mother to see if her parents would take the kids for the weekend. Then she booked a remote cabin out of town where she and Trent liked to go. Sara hoped to find the courage to discuss all this so she and Trent could start building a healthier relationship.

Keys

Jingle jangle the keys wrangle
We each hold our ring of keys
Keys lock and keys open
One opens the door to the house
Or locks others out
One opens the mind
Or shuts out thoughts
And yet another opens the heart
to allow sharing of life
Or shuts one off from even those they love

How can one life hold so many keys
Who do you share the keys with

Family
each has the key to the front door of the house
Yet seldom
perhaps
to the minds of those who reside within

In times past
my keys were used to lock and block
keep others out
I thought this was the prudent way to face the world

Yet now
keys open
doorways
homes
the mind
the heart
Presenting a completely different way of living

My comfort now is open and sharing
Do you want me to send you a key

Anticipation

Clouds were building in the heavens. Billowy clouds, piled on top of one another, reaching high into the sky. They changed from white fluffy clouds to dark clouds, heavy with moisture. The farmer and his wife gazed into the sky; then at each other. He said to her, "if there's no moisture today, we'll lose our crop."

She wiped her brow. "We still have the chickens, flour in the barrel, and I've put up the last of the vegetables."

"Don't be so damned optimistic, woman! We've reached the breaking point. There needs to be rain today." He turned and stomped off toward the machine shed.

She shook her head and turned toward the house. As she shut the kitchen door, she heard the distant rumble of thunder and thought, *Dear God, please let there be rain.*

What Should We Do With the Body

"What should we do with the body?" said Shane.

"Shhh."

His father glanced around before responding. "We need to dispose of the body somewhere where no one will find it."

"But Dad, don't you think we should notify someone?"

"Son. Do you realize what you're suggesting? It would take days, maybe weeks, for someone to arrive here. The body will stink and most surely bring trouble to cousin Collin. The family businesses will be shuttered. You need to do as I say. Do you understand?"

Shane's shoulders slumped.

"Yes, sir."

"Good. Locate a spot in the back forty where we can bury the body. I'll bring it out by wagon late in the afternoon and we can bury it before sun-down. We need to get this wood moved, so it's ready when Shay comes to pick up his load. We don't want anyone messing around this boxcar."

"How much lumber is Shay picking up?"

"Just one wagon load. I'll help, and we should be able to have the wood stacked over by the tree before Shay arrives. Then we can move the liquor and get it stored in the shed. We'll finish unloading the rest tomorrow."

After they stacked the lumber and moved the liquor to the shed, Brendan climbed into the boxcar and headed to the lump wrapped in oilcloth. He pulled back the covering. The man appeared to be in his mid-thirties, dressed in slacks, a white shirt and a tweed vest which coordinated with his slacks. Brendan was about to turn away when a folded sheet of paper caught his eye. He picked up the paper and carefully opened it.

It read, "Dear Cuz. Sorry for the delivery. I had no choice. It was him or our business. I took nothing off the body so it couldn't be traced to me. You're far enough away. It shouldn't matter. Next shipment will be simpler. Sincerely, Collin."

Brendan turned back to the man. He saw a pocket watch peeking out from under the man's vest. He carefully removed it and dropped the watch in his jeans pocket. When he lifted the vest, he saw a pistol in the man's belt. Gingerly, he removed the gun and placed it beside the body. His pockets were bare, and the man wore no jewelry. Brendan stood just as Shane was entering the car.

"Son, this is serious business. He was a revenuer out to shutter our business and take away Collin. Here, hide this gun in the shed. We have no choice but to deal with this immediately. Why don't you take the horse and start digging a trench? I'll join you once Shay picks up his lumber."

Unable to comprehend everything his father was saying, Shane stood there looking first at his father and then at the dead body.

"Get goin' boy. We got serious work to do here."

"Yes sir," said Shane.

He spun around, jumped down from the car, and went to locate the horse. He was happy his father assigned him a task away from the body. Never had he been in the presence of a dead person before, and he didn't feel comfortable at all around the man still in the wagon. After locating an enormous tree in the back forty, he dug a deep pit for the body. Then sat down with his back against the tree, trying to calm his nerves as he waited for his father to arrive.

The memories of this event never left Shane and changed him forever. He knew of the family's success after they staked their claims from the land lottery. It was uncommon for family members to gain claims in the same area, but they had. They had good fun setting up the land and building gathering spots. Shay ran the lumber operation. Wood was scarce in the Dakotas, so Brendan's operation to bring in train loads of lumber from Chicago provided the materials for the new buildings. When residents came to the dance hall, they relished the liquor, which unknown to them had been hidden amongst the lumber transported from Chicago. While at the dance hall they enjoyed fresh homemade ice cream as well. The family experienced a good life. Being so far from civilization, lawmen seldom visited them. They continued their business operations and opened the first newspaper, a school, several other dealings, and eventually built a church.

Shane knew his family's hard work, entrepreneurial skills, connections in both the Dakotas and Chicago all played into their success. So did burying the body. Shane often wondered about the man's family; the people who cared about him and loved him. Did they wonder what happened to him? How did their lives continue without him? His own family's success and the guilt of the man's losses initially drove Shane away from the Dakotas. He moved further west and seldom wrote home. He'd learned about how prohibition affected different locations within the United States, providing him a better understanding of why his father acted as he had. There were days he missed his family, yet when he thought of them he could not escape the memories of the man lying wrapped in the oil cloth.

Trunk Sale

Sharon smiled as she stood, surveying the boxes piled around her. Tomorrow is the trunk sale, an opportunity for her to help with fund-raising efforts for the Children's Hospital and a time where she can gather with her women friends. How different she felt about this year's event compared to the first year she participated.

Back then, she lived in a perpetual state of sadness. She'd felt abandoned and didn't know where to turn. A drunk driver had killed her Samuel. One moment in time had changed her entire life. As she spiraled deeper and deeper into depression, she withdrew more into herself. She worked as a bookkeeper for a small business, and kept to herself. Once a week, she went to a counseling session. After arriving home, she often sat in the dark staring out the window, sobbing about her life. Samuel had been the bright spot who brought joy into her days. Since his death, her anger grew as she judged how deprived she was as a child, and now deprived of love and a chance for happiness as a woman. She directed her anger at people from her past and those around her; angry because no one saw she was hurting. No one was ever there for her. There was no one to rescue her from herself and her negative thoughts. Anger was the emotion she carried with her most days. This was her life.

One day, after many counseling sessions, the therapist retorted, "You, Sharon, will not become well until you crawl out of yourself. You are hurting. So are many others. Go to the Children's Hospital; walk the halls; study the faces of the family members sitting there. Then glance into some rooms. There, you will discover many who have relinquished hope. Give of yourself to them. If you determine you can't manage to do this, here's the number of a woman who organizes fund-raising efforts for the hospital. Perhaps you might help her."

The therapist pulled a business card from her desk drawer and handed it to Sharon.

"When you return next week, I want to hear what you've done for the children. Then we'll discuss your life."

Sharon stood, took the card from the therapist, with shoulders slumped, she turned and shuffled out the office. When she unlocked her vehicle and sat in the seat, thoughts flooded her mind. *Who does she assume she is talking with when she speaks to me in such a manner? I pay her for her time and she's supposed to be helping me. Should I cancel my next appointment?*

Sharon shook her head trying to clear her thoughts; she turned the key in the ignition, and drove home. Sitting at the window, in her chair, she couldn't dismiss the words from her head, words that she needed to crawl out of herself. It was true, she had no friends or outside interests. Most days, she seemed miserable and lethargic. Exhausted and weary of thinking, she trudged down the hallway to her bedroom. She considered calling the woman.

Sharon remembers it like yesterday. It was three years ago when she made the first phone call. Pam was energetic and excited to hear someone wanted to help with the fundraising. She provided the date for the event, suggestions of welcome donations for the sale, and told Sharon after setting up her stuff, she could help at the check-out table. Sharon hung up the phone, wondering what she had gotten herself into. She reviewed the donations notes she'd written and determined this might be one way to finally clear out some of Samuel's clothing items from her house. The next couple of evenings after work, Sharon collected items from various closets and set up a pile in the living room.

Saturday arrived, and Sharon drove to the event. She set out her donations on the table. A bubbly woman approached her, extended her hand and said, "I'm Pam. And you are…?"

"Hi, my name is Sharon."

"Great! We're glad to have you join the team. Come with me to meet the others."

With that, Pam was off, leaving Sharon little choice but to follow her. They made introductions. Sharon was polite, yet avoided any conversation. Pam lead her over to the cash area and explained how everything worked. Sharon barely responded.

Finally, Pam stopped and said, "Sharon, what is going on? The participants attending today's event, both the volunteers and the shoppers, are excited to be helping and to be surrounded by others also committed to the Children's Hospital. Is something wrong? And are you up for interacting with the public today?"

Sharon had no recollection of what compelled her to tell this woman her story, but she recounted the events of Samuel's death and how she seemed dead without him. Pam's empathy and understanding appeared sincere, and Sharon felt herself relaxing and less anxious about those around her. She assured Pam she could handle the sales counter. The people started arriving. The energy level was high and people were genuinely interested in supporting the hospital. In fact, many paid more than the actual price for their purchases. Sharon couldn't recall experiencing such passion regarding helping another in her lifetime and became wrapped up in the excitement surrounding the day's event.

After returning home, the dark shroud of gloom wrapped itself around her once again. As she sat in the dark and stared out the window, she tried to comprehend what was different about today. She trudged off to bed with no answers.

At counseling, she recounted the events of Saturday's sale. Her counselor encouraged her to spend more time with other people, to confront her fears and find nuggets of happy times to weave into her history. Sharon doubted if these actions would work for her, yet acknowledged Saturday while at the trunk sale, she didn't reflect on feeling sad. She left her counseling session after agreeing to at least look for happy memories and start a notebook to record them. This tool would become a reference resource for her when she got depressed. Might this work for her? Sharon didn't know, but decided she should try.

One day when pondering her memories, she recognized how different she felt now when with others than how she'd felt before. She quickly blamed it on "the others," but as she questioned herself, she realized people prefer to spend time with those who were happy, and it had been a long time since she'd been happy. She swallowed hard and wrote in her journal she had been driving other people away, which deepened her sense of loneliness and abandonment. Then she wrote, but it is my fault; and I can change my attitude.

Sharon continued working with the women who support the Children's Hospital and met with several of them regularly. They had become her friends. She appeared lighter, happier, and even talked about the past and shared pleasant memories.

Sharon grabbed her purse as she ran out the door. She was excited as she considered, how greatly her life changed in a few short years. *I can't believe it and I can't wait to get to the trunk sale.*

Bougainvillea

Bougainvillea plants explode with color
Thin petals
Each bloom tightly holds four to six petals together
Two white dots fill the center of each as identifying
marks for the species
Some tower to the sky growing against the house
Others fill large areas of the garden
Whichever, they fill their space with color and gaiety
Colors vary depending upon plant
The blossoms dry
then flutter to the ground
They swirl in the air
ultimately landing below
Like tissue paper
scattered and left behind
After the celebration

Memories and Bougainvillea

The yard represents life
Family visited for two weeks
House filled with laughter
Children played games
ran in the garden
Shared cooking experiences
A glass of wine
enjoyed in the evenings
Tomorrow's adventures planned
Car loaded
Family departed
Time flies

Memories are left
scattered around
Different shades and hews
Much like my bougainvillea tissue flowers

The Auction

Charlene and Ted prowled around town, checking out specialty shops and an estate warehouse location. While there, they noted several pieces of interest but weren't prepared to purchase anything. When they returned to the store two days later, both items had "SOLD" signs posted on them.

Ted signed up for the business mailing list. Charlene thought little about this. Every couple of weeks they received an email, listing new items in the warehouse or boasting an estate sale. After returning to the shop to view a specific art piece only to find it sold, Charlene ignored the emails.

One morning Ted said, "Can you be ready to leave the house by 8:45? I've RSVP'd for a private auction."

"Ok," said Charlene. "Is there something special you're considering?"

"Not particularly. The listing sounded interesting, and I thought it would be a fun outing. Let's grab a quick breakfast and be on our way. Please hurry!"

"Sure. You won't have to wait for me."

The drive took them through neighborhoods they had not visited before. They arrived at the address and parked their car. Before they approached the driveway, a shuttle picked them up to drive them up the long approach. As they departed the shuttle, the driver told them he would be available to return them to their car anytime. Out of the vehicle, they stood and gazed around. The house sat atop a hill. The driveway opened into an impressive courtyard area. Those hosting the auction had set up tents and chairs in advance. Someone greeted them, had them sign in, and gave them their number for the event. The greeter explained the auction processes for the day and invited them to walk through the house and grounds, review the items, and select items of interest. Staff would move larger items to an outside table. Snacks, fruit, small sandwiches, and drinks, including beer or wine were available, and they were told to help themselves.

With the front-door wide open the home radiated a welcome atmosphere. The home's entrance door was a massive wooden door decorated with a three-dimensional stylized wooden leaf sweeping from the top to mid-point. Charlene, captivated by the stain-glass artwork built in above the entry, didn't see the beauty of the door until Ted pointed it out later.

Upon entering the foyer, the first thing which caught Charlene's eye was a wooden music stand holding two wooden recorders. Art flanked the walls on either side of the doorway and multiple short hallways conjoined in the foyer. They took the hallway to the right. Several large rooms awaited them down this hallway. One room was a bedroom, where personal toiletries, lingerie and clothing were on display with several pieces of furniture. Ted and Charlene moved through this space quickly into the library. Books, records and collectibles were all priced and lay out for people to view.

From the library, they retraced their steps to the foyer, selected another hallway, and entered the kitchen. All the cupboards were open; all countertops had items grouped together. Beautiful crystal and china sets adorned the countertops. The cupboards housed mixed silver and a few odd pieces of china. Pottery was displayed in multiple rooms. The kitchen opened into the dining room and living room. Large pieces of art hung on the walls.

They filled the living room spaces with tables displaying small art, pottery, collectibles and glass cases filled with jewelry. An elegant violin lay on the floor in an open case.

Charlene and Ted stepped onto the back patio. There in the fresh air, they surveyed the landscaping and various large pots, also for sale. There were few shoppers outdoors. They took their time. On the patio, they found several large blue pots to their liking.

Charlene said, "Did you see the Koi painting in the first bedroom?"

"Yes. It was nicely done," said Ted.

"I enjoyed it. The blue background contained enough flourishes of white and lighter blue shades to create the sense of water movement. Then the splashes of color twisted in different shapes presented Koi swimming. Do you like it enough to purchase?"

"I liked it, but I don't want to acquire more art of that size. We still have pieces we own and haven't hung," said Ted.

Charlene sighed. "You're right. I'm returning to the house to view the remaining rooms and discover if I missed anything on the first pass."

"Me too."

Inside the house again, Charlene discovered the art room and immediately felt at home. It was a large room with amazing light, workspaces, and cupboards. As she walked around the room, she scrutinized the vast assortment of supplies and recognized at least one owner created many types of art. It was then, she realized it was the owner's initials on the Koi piece she'd seen in the bedroom. Ted joined her in the art room, just as Charlene picked up some Gouache paint and a book on color blending.

"I need to add these to our table."

Ted said, "Good idea. I've had the pots moved from the back patio."

"Remember the coffee mug I pointed out in the kitchen," said Charlene.

"Uh-ha."

Well, I'll pick it up on my way out. Meet you under the tents," said Charlene.

Ted and Charlene took seats and watched others, reviewing items selected by someone else.

Charlene chuckled and Ted asked, "What's funny?"

"You see the large abstract piece in bright colors, highlighted in black? I can't believe more than one person is interested in such a piece of art. I see a woman sprawled on the bed, dead or passed out. It was in the last bedroom, hanging over the bed. I found it a strange piece of art."

Ted laughed. "It looks like an abstract of city buildings."

They both laughed and agreed, this is a good example of what makes art so personal. They talked about several of the large pieces they had seen. Many were contemporary; some interesting, but not compatible with their décor.

Ted said, "Did you like the pair of paintings hanging in the living room? I think you should go back and check them out. Let me know what you think."

Charlene returned to the house and found the two paintings. A nearby larger ceramic geometric wall piece had dominated the space, garnering her earlier attention. Upon closer examination, the paintings were very modern, but the colors were right and the pieces displayed movement. It felt like someone captured the wind in autumn colors. They were complimentary and being sold as a pair.

Charlene returned to Ted and said. "They are great. I can't believe I missed them the first time."

"I believe they'll work in the space where we want something large."

"Yes, but weren't they expensive?"

"I've been pondering the same question. Even if we purchased a large print or two, and had them framed, we would have even more invested. And these are original paintings."

"So true! I think they'd look splendid in our house. Before you select them, we need to discuss how high we'd be willing to bid, if someone else wants them as well.

They figured out what their top dollar would be and Ted returned to the house to put their number on the two pieces.

It was approaching noon and the host announced the rules for the pre-auction sales. Everyone had selected items on tables with their numbers. All were encouraged to peruse these tables and move anything they were interested in from someone else's table to a front table. The auction would only contain items from the front tables. Items on the other tables would be sold to the person who originally selected them at the beginning bid price marked on each item, plus ten percent.

A woman moved one item Charlene had selected to the front table. It was the oversized coffee mug in bright royal blue with whimsical cats painted on the cup, Charlene had fetched from the kitchen. Charlene liked the shape of the mug, liked the color, and was attracted to cats. The creator of the cup is rather famous for her feline designs, but that was lost on Charlene. Yet she had to bid several times on the coffee mug to obtain it.

Ted was surprised Charlene bid against the other woman several times. In the end, the mug went home with Charlene.

Someone else had selected a large blue ceramic pot and saucer that Ted bid on.

The auction process went quickly, items paid for, then packed into the vehicle. The large pots, plus two large art pieces, proved to be a challenge for Ted and Charlene but with a little repositioning, everything was in the vehicle and they left for home. While driving, they talked about what they had seen. The estate contained an amazing collection of art.

Ted said, "Did you notice they only had one TV? I think we would have gotten on well with them."

"I missed that. But you can't watch television and read books or create art. You know, I felt like this could be our house."

"You're not planning on us moving, are you?" said Ted.

"No. No. I don't mean the house, but the inside, the stuff. Someday after we die, our home could host a similar sale; all our belongings displayed for others to go through. The kids are interested in so few of our possessions."

"You might be right," said Ted.

Charlene pondered this thought for several days. She was grateful the family chose an auction so the property or art could be re-homed versus going to the landfill.

Charlene had such conflicting thoughts about the event. Initially, upon entering the house an eerie sensation overcame her. She felt like the previous owners' lives had been exposed to everyone as their possessions were displayed on counters and tables, with small price tags showing the opening bid price. Nothing appeared too personal to be on display. She recognized at some future time her home would look like this. Treasures she and Ted collected throughout their years together may mean little to the children, and thus their lives would similarly end on display, for all to pick through for purchase or to pass over. Uncomfortable with this notion, Charlene made a quick mental note to reflect on what things were lurking in her home. Yet, when in the art-room, she experienced different feelings. There, again, she realized this could be her stuff one day. She smiled at the prospect of someone finding inspiration among her things.

A Morning in My Life

By Shamu

Note: A short story written from the perspective of a cat.

I uncurl from my sleep and stretch, allowing my front paws to touch your arm. You're still sound asleep and I'm hungry. I knead on your arm, but you just roll away. That will never do. I jump to my feet after stretching and approach your face. I butt my head against yours. With groggy eyes, you glance at me and rub my ears. Still, you don't arise. I decided you must be told what to do, so I talk.

"Oh, Shamu. Why do you insist on such early mornings? Okay. I'll get up."

You slowly grab your robe to go downstairs. I'm way ahead of you, talking all the way. You set out fresh food for me, then fix your coffee. I pick at my food, then saunter around the kitchen looking out the patio doors. You will never allow me outside. I'd like to join you on an outing.

I stretch out on the couch to watch you until you come and also sit on the couch. I roll over and approach so I can sit on your lap. You never sit for long, but I want to be near you.

Your daughter arrives, and I approach her. She will pick me up and cuddle with me. I purr and butt my head against her. She's grand and I love her, but you are still my preference.

I Hated That Smile

Immediately, I knew someone had put me in my place. I liked to be the character who caught others off guard and caused them to stammer and then be silent. People enjoyed my jovial attitude and easy banter. The tips I received were proof of how well I could interact with others.

Friday evening started like any other since COVID raged in our land, shutting down the bustle of tourist activity. Even the locals stayed away as the governor encouraged people to remain at home. The restaurant closed for a while and I, like my co-workers, survived on our weekly unemployment checks. After what seemed like forever, the stay-at-home restrictions were removed and the locals moved throughout town. I could return to work. It was different. Outdoor dining became acceptable, even for fine dining establishments like ours. The owner set up large white tents and got outdoor heaters. Bantering with locals differed from with tourists, yet it overjoyed me to be working and interacting with individuals again. One can only stay home alone for so long. As another phase of COVID crossed the nation, our governor, eager to re-open the state to travelers, enacted a mandatory face mask order for all businesses, even for out-door gatherings. Back at work again, I felt fortunate. Many businesses were slow to re-open, or operated with skeleton staff and only with advance appointments. As a state, we kept our case numbers in check and the tourists trickled into town again. The autumn colors, falling leaves and cooler temperatures lured more travelers to return. And return they did. Apparently, the country was as tired of social distancing as I.

Back to the evening of my story. It was chilly outside; business was bustling. We required reservations, and we were at capacity. They sauntered in, confirmed their reservation, and sat at one of my tables. They were one of my first tables in the tent. I turned on the heater closest to them and then another. It was obvious; they knew one another well as I watched them talking, laughing and gesturing throughout their conversation. One couple ordered wine and the other did not. None of them seemed to notice this difference as they gave their drink orders and carried on with their conversation. I returned with drinks and answered a few questions about various menu dishes. Both ladies ordered our Apple and Butternut Squash soup. It's always been one of my favorites, but many customers are cautious of ordering this item and seldom dare to try something different. The men ordered salads. Main entrées were ordered, and I left them to their conversations. The kitchen had their starters prepared, and I saw my assistant bring the plated salads to the table. Everyone at the table watched in amazement as my assistant served the soup. A white bowl with an oversized lip, containing a small deep well, was placed in front of each women. The bowls were garnished with pecans and pickled winter squash. A dollop of vanilla ricotta lay at the bottom of the well, awaiting the soup. The server then picked up the long, elegant white porcelain vessel and carefully poured the soup atop the vanilla ricotta. I stood back and watched the presentation. It was amazing, as always, and impressed everyone at the table. The ladies tasted the soup. I didn't need to inquire if they found it acceptable, as their reactions were obvious.

Another table was seated, a couple that were celebrating a special occasion or in the pangs of a new love, though they weren't young. This table immediately ordered a bottle of wine and several cocktails as they settled into their chairs. Frequently, they reached across the table, touching hands or occasionally kissing. My mind was already calculating a good tip from this couple. They interrupted my thoughts by asking for my recommendations for dinner. How different this table was from my first, where everyone knew precisely what they wished to order. I suggested the soup. The lady hesitated.

"I don't know. Squash is not my favorite."

I said, "It is my favorite. But don't take my word for it. Let's ask the table over there. The ladies both ordered soup."

I turned to the first table. "Excuse me. I'm sorry for interrupting, but would you mind telling this couple what you think of the soup."

I couldn't discern who said what as they both responded.

"Delicious!"

"Definitely order this. It is amazing."

I winked and said, "I'll square up with you later."

Both women laughed and were beaming. I recognized I would receive an excellent tip from this table as well, even though they weren't drinking much.

The next table seated was a party of six. They came from the bar to their table and immediately ordered cocktails. My original party received their dinner plates and everyone was satisfied with their entrées. Conversation flowed easily at their table, with short bursts of laughter filling the air.

`I returned to my party of six to take their orders, and when they had hesitation concerning the soup, I turned to my first table of the evening again.

"I'm sorry to interrupt your conversation again, but would you mind sharing what you thought of the soup tonight?"

One lady gave a thumbs up and nodded her head, the other commented, "It was delicious. By all means, try it."

"Thank you." I winked and said, "I'll square up with you later."

Everyone laughed.

I didn't give it another thought and continued to ensure I satisfied all my tables with their meals, filled drink glasses, and then tried to ply them with dessert. My first table declined the dessert offer, instead ordering hot drinks around the table. I served the drinks and dropped off the bill, received a charge card, and returned to the table. One woman inquired as to how I would compensate them.

Being quick on my feet, I said, "Here is how it works. You need to return tomorrow morning and plan on being here for twelve hours."

She laughed and said, "I haven't worked a twelve-hour day in years."

I continued, "Well, we have a crew here to film our next advertisements. You'll be in an ad for us and become famous. Imagine that, you could be famous."

I smiled, thinking I had done a marvelous job of dealing with this and still remained being in charge.

She quickly said, "I don't think you understand. I am already famous and don't need to do a film ad."

Everyone at the table broke into laughter. I didn't know what to say. I glanced around and saw my assistant with that wicked grin. I hated that grin! She knew I'd been bested, and she wouldn't let me forget this evening easily.

I walked back to the kitchen with her following me. In the kitchen, she said, "For once, you didn't have a comeback, did you? Do you even know who they are?"

"No! Please go back and start clearing the table and just leave me alone right now? I don't know those individuals. How can they be famous?"

As she walked away, I could see the foursome had left their table. They were still laughing as they sauntered into the parking lot, leaving me to ponder the evening and if I should know who these people were.

Trapped

Sasha and Theodore were chasing each other throughout the house. They would tumble and roll on the floor, often intertwining. When they heard the doorbell, they dashed under the sofa.

They watched and listened. Then they cringed. Mary had just opened the door and Pamela entered. As they moved further under the sofa, they stared at each other. They felt safe crouching against the back wall. They lay flat as possible on the floor and listened. Maybe Pamela was here to pick up Mary, and they'd go somewhere else to play.

No such luck today. Pamela jerked off her jacket and threw it on the stairs, along with a bag she had brought with her.

"What should we do today? Let's have a tea-party." said Mary.

"Umm… I don't know."

Mary said, "Let's watch cartoons till we figure out what we want to do."

She ran across the room to turn on her TV. Mickey Mouse and friends were playing.

The girls plopped on the sofa and absorbed the sights and sounds coming from the television.

Sasha and Theodore relaxed a bit and crept closer to the edge of the sofa. Sasha whispered to Theodore, "Let's get out of the room and hide somewhere else."

"I'll follow you. Just be careful. You don't want Pamela to see you," said Theodore.

Of course, Theodore and Sasha communicated in cat language, which is translated for you so you can understand what they are saying.

When Sasha reached the front corner of the sofa, she looked around. The girls were talking and laughing and she couldn't see their feet. She darted out from under the sofa and raced up the stairs. Theodore was right behind her. Part way up the stairs, Sasha heard the shriek.

"Oh, there they are!" said Pamela. She jumped up from the sofa to chase the cats.

She stopped, turned, and put her hands on her hips.

"I want to play baby dolls with the cats. Oh Mary, that will be fun." said Pamela.

"Oh no! I remember how horrible the experience was the last time they played this game. Run. You hide in one room, I'll hide in another. Maybe they won't be able to catch us," said Theodore.

They didn't wait to hear Mary's response. They each ran into a different bedroom and hid under the bed. The girls were racing up the stairs behind Sasha and Theodore. Pamela darted into the room after Theodore and peered under the bed. She saw his green eyes glaring back at her. He saw her big, toothy grin and hissed at her as she reached under the bed.

"Now kitty. Be nice. We just want to play with you," said Pamela.

Theodore swatted at Pamela, then ran to the corner where he crouched down and glowered at her.

"Bad kitty!"

Pamela reached under the bed using large, sweeping movements where she caught a hold of Theodore's tail and pulled him out from under the bed. His claws scraped against the floor and he howled.

Mary, who had Sasha in her arms, came running into the room.

"What is going on in here?" said Mary.

Pamela proudly held up Theodore.

"I caught the bad kitty. See what he did to my arm."

Mary looked at Theodore and shook her head.

"You're not supposed to scratch people."

Mary failed to understand when Theodore tried to tell her how mean Pamela was.

"Come on, the baby clothes are in my bedroom," said Mary.

To no avail, Sasha and Theodore twisted and wiggled, trying to get free from the girls. After they tied the bonnets under the kitty's chins and had the gowns wrapped around their bodies, Pamela took leashes out of her bag.

"I think we need to put them on leashes and tightly hook them onto the pram so they can't jump out and escape like they did the last time.

Sasha turned toward Theodore and could see he was seething. His ears were flat back and his eyes were little slits. The girls strapped both cats into the stroller under tight leashes.

Then they strolled around the block. Other children would call out to them. Pamela would encourage others to come look at their babies.

Sasha lay as still as possible. The bonnet had her ears flattened against her head and was tightly tied under her chin. It hurt her to move her head. Theodore had crawled under the blanket and curled himself into the tightest ball possible. Before crawling under the blanket, he had one final thing to say to Sasha.

"I've got to hide my face. If the other Tommys spot me, the heckling will be nonstop."

Sasha said, "Ok. I can't move. I hurt."

Mary and Pamela chatted and giggled as they walked their "children" around the block.

"Oh. They are so cute," said Pamela.

"Yes, they are. I love my cuddly kittens," said Mary.

Once back inside the house, Mary lifted first Sasha out of the prams. She snuggled her as she removed the gown and took the bonnet off Sasha's head. Sasha fiercely shook her head and jumped from Mary's arms. Theodore was next. Pamela wasn't in such a hurry to remove the clothes, and Theodore leapt from her arms to the sofa. There he stood, howling. He let out a loud cry after every step Pamela made towards him. Mary approached and picked him up.

"Come on, big boy. Let mama get these clothes off you."

Theodore became limp and compliant in Mary's arm as she removed the gown and untied the bonnet. Then she bent down and carefully set Theodore on the floor, rubbing his ears.

"You go play now," said Mary.

Sasha and Theodore met in the kitchen. He was still steaming.

"This will never happen to me again. Mary is okay, but her friend will never touch me again. I'm leaving. Are you coming with me?"

"Leaving? What do you mean?" said Sasha.

"I'm going to leave. Someone will be careless when they either enter or exit the house, and the next time someone dawdles, I'm slipping out the door. Are you coming with me?"

Sasha walked around the kitchen, rubbing against the table legs.

"Come on, Sasha. Are you with me? How many times will you let that Pamela kid treat you like this? It's humiliating," said Theodore.

"Well, I, hum, I don't know."

"Suit yourself. You're either in or not. But I'm outta here!"

Theodore jumped onto the windowsill and sat with his front feet firmly planted under him, head held high, staring out the window.

Theodore wouldn't engage in any further conversation with Sasha, no matter how hard she tried. She paced from one room to the next, unable to decide what to do. She loved Mary, she really did. But she also loved Theodore and couldn't imagine life in the house without him to talk with, romp with, and on cold days to curl together in one large ball to stay warm. What would she do? Perhaps she wouldn't have to decide. Maybe Theodore would forget about leaving.

A commotion arose in the front room as Pamala was preparing to leave. Theodore climbed behind the hat stand in the foyer after jumping from the window.

Sasha came over by him and rubbed up beside him. Pamela put on her jacket, and Mary opened the front door.

Pamela said, "I forgot my bag upstairs. Be back in a minute." She ran up the stairs and Mary followed her, leaving the door open.

"Now's the time for my escape. Are you coming with me or not?" said Theodore.

"I guess," said Sasha.

They darted out the door and skirted beneath the shrubbery. The air was fresh. This was an unfamiliar experience for Sasha. She wasn't on a leash, confined in the baby stroller or gripped in someone's arms. As she stretched and smelled the afternoon air, she felt liberated. When she saw a bug, she jumped and moved cautiously through the foliage. She did not know what other critters were or how they might hurt her. Theodore was much braver as he scouted out the plantings and undergrowth near the house. They both heard the girls come out of the house as they planned their next afternoon play date. Theodore refused to look at them.

He turned his back and said, "Good-riddens to life trapped in the house."

Sasha continued to stare at Mary and Pamela. She didn't like Pamela much, but Mary. Mary was a different story. She slept on Mary's bed and liked the soft comforter. She enjoyed when Mary would softly rub her ears. She knew she was going to miss Mary.

Theodore moved around the corner of the house and was scoping out the backyard. He ran to the old oak tree and started climbing it.

"Come on Sasha. The view from up here is amazing. You'll love it."

Sasha joined him. She could peer into the bedroom windows from the tree and also see the neighbor's backyard. She liked the vantage point in the tree, but had to admit, a bird startled her when it flew into the tree and quickly retreated after seeing her. Why would a bird fear her?

They romped and played throughout the afternoon. The sun was setting, and the temperatures were dropping, making the evening cool.

Sasha stretched. She said, "I'm hungry. Where's the food?"

"Sasha, we have to find our own food. I'll go get something for us tonight. Then tomorrow, you'll need to hunt your own food. You stay here. I'll be back."

With those words, Theodore was gone. Sasha sat crouched close to the ground. She didn't know what to think. Sasha missed the warmth of the house. She missed Mary reaching down to rub her ears, and she missed the food always available in the dish on the floor beside the patio window. Her stomach growled. The outside noises were frightening her. She didn't notice Theodore return until he was right beside her. He dropped a small grey thing by her feet. She jumped.

"Oh, it's you. I'm glad you're back. What is this?"

Theodore said, "That, dear Sasha, is dinner. I can only catch one mouse at a time, so we must share."

"Yuk! That thing has fur on it. I can see its eyes. I've never eaten something like this before."

"Sasha. It's this mouse, or nothing."

Sasha started crying uncontrollably. Through her shaking and her tears, Theodore could barely understand her.

"I don't like it here. I'm hungry. I'm cold. I'm scared. I want to go home."

"Sasha. We pulled off the great escape. I thought you wanted to join me. I told you, I'm not going back there. Never will I have to tolerate Pamela's abuse again. Never!" said Theodore.

"I didn't know what to expect with you. I can't do this. Please take me home," said Sasha as she stood there shaking.

"Sasha, I'll walk you back to the house. I'll even scratch on the door to get someone's attention. But I won't allow them to see me, and I won't come in. Is this what you want?"

Sasha rubbed against Theodore and said, "Yes."

Slowly, the two walked back toward the house. The front porch light was on. Sasha brushed against Theodore one last time. When he looked at her, she couldn't discern if it was deep sadness or disgust she saw in his eyes. He jumped against the door and it rattled. He heard footsteps in the house and he ran off into the shrubbery. Sasha watched him as he ran away. Mary's mother came to the door and opened it. She peered out toward the street, looking first to the right and then to the left. She shook her head and turned back toward the house. It was then, she saw Sasha pressed against the door. She reached down, and swooped Sasha into her arms.

"Mary, Sasha is home."

Permission Granted

I give myself permission

I give myself permission to write.
I give myself permission to write badly.
I give myself permission to write things that make no sense.
I give myself permission to write random thoughts, which fly through my mind.
I give myself permission to read.
I give myself permission to read stories I find to be funny, sad, or anything in between.
I give myself permission to not need all the answers.
I give myself permission to be wrong.
I give myself permission to love with abandon.
I give myself permission to enjoy every moment of my life.
I give myself permission to explore life and all it has to offer.
I give myself permission to cry or be emotional.
I give myself permission to say my feelings are hurt.
I give myself permission to have feelings others might not understand.
I give myself permission to enjoy friendships.
I give myself permission to not meet others expectations.
I give myself permission to spend time on my interests, cooking, writing, art, gardening, friends.
I give myself permission to wear the clothes I like.

I give myself permission to walk away from relationships that are harmful or hurtful to me.
I give myself permission to be silly.
I give myself permission to say 'NO'.
I give myself permission to experience feelings even I don't understand.
I give myself permission to be protective of "my" own time.
I give myself permission to enjoy travel.
I give myself permission to enjoy my home.
I give myself permission to spend time with whom I please.

In some ways, this sounds selfish – yet in reality, I recognize the freedom to acknowledge permission to do things I previously questioned. I spent far too many years thinking I had to make others happy, or do what was expected of me.
I wonder, is this part of the **when I'm an old woman...** phase of life. Others have written of reaching an age when they realize they don't have to please anyone else, and feel this immense freedom to simply be themselves. I think it is a wonderful time. I suspect my mother would have wished she could have given this to me at a younger age. I certainly wish I could have figured out how to give it to my children, but realize during those years, I myself was way too busy worrying about meeting everyone else's expectations, thus these concepts were lost of me.

Oh, happy day! I'm old enough to know better.

Last Day On Earth

Megan awoke to a sound similar to a swarm of mosquitos lifting into the morning sky. She jumped out of bed and pulled back the window blinds. The sun was just rising on the horizon, but today it was emitting a dull orange shadow on the earth. In the murky light, Megan could identify the carrier's grey shape lifting into the sky. Similar transports had been leaving twice a day, morning, and evening, for weeks. Every day, the sun was less bright, and the air felt heavier.

Megan ran down the hall, threw open the door, went over to the bed and shook Jamie, her sister.

"Jamie. Jamie, wake up! We must get up and leave here. Pack your backpack and meet me in the kitchen for breakfast. Hurry!"

"Oh, Megan, what's the rush?" said Jamie.

"Come on. Don't give me any crap today. Just get dressed and hurry downstairs."

Megan returned to her room. She threw open her closet and grabbed a pair of jeans, a lightweight long-sleeved shirt, a lightweight windbreaker and her tennis shoes. Her backpack, already full, was by the door. Before leaving her room, she stopped to take one more look around. Her books lay on the night table beside the bed. Photos of her parents, and of her with friends lined the shelf over her bed. A tear slowly formed and ran down her check. She wiped it away with her sleeve, shook her head, turned, and ran down the stairs.

Jamie entered the room just as Megan put two cereal bowls on the table.

"You're serious, aren't you?" said Jamie.

"What do you mean?" said Megan.

"You got your backpack by the door with your jacket. We're really going to leave? How can we? This is home. It's all I've ever known," said Jamie. Her voice quivered, and she started shaking.

Megan walked over and put her arms around her sister. They stood in the kitchen, sobbing. Megan took a step back and put her hands-on Jamie's shoulders.

"Hon, I know this is hard. I know you're scared. So am I. We have no choice. I don't have any knowledge of our destination and I can't promise we'll even like it. But I can tell you, we can't stay here. I promised mom and dad I would make sure you and I stayed together. We've got seats on the evening transport—together! Let's have breakfast and then spend today walking around town and checking out the places where we used to hang."

Jamie shrugged her shoulders, hung her head a little and murmured, "Okay."

The girls finished breakfast, and Jamie got up to do the dishes.

Megan said, "Don't bother with the dishes. No one will know we left them."

The girls let out a weak laugh, picked up their backpacks and headed out the backdoor.

"I suppose you're going to tell me we don't have to lock the door either," said Jamie.

"Well, I hadn't thought of it, but you have a novel idea. Why bother?"

The street was silent. Gone were the cars, formerly buzzing down the street. No children were playing in the yards, yelling to one another or whooping it up when someone scored. Even the birds and animals were gone. An orange haze filled the air. Nothing you could touch, but it hung in the air like a gauze you had to peer through. Everything looked out of focus and yet strangely familiar.

Jamie shuffled along behind Megan. Megan looked back. When she saw Jamie lagging behind her, she called out, "Come on! I want to walk around town one last time."

"Why bother. Nothing is the same. I want to remember this place, my home, the way it was, not like this." She sank down to the curb, wrapped her arms around her knees and dropped her head.

Megan walked back to her sister. She sat down beside her and put her arms around Jamie's shoulders as they stared down the street. Megan realized Jamie was right. What's the point of walking through a town practically deserted and quieter than death? Megan shivered a little as she realized they would be dead if they missed the last transport. She stood and reached out for Jamie's hand.

"Come on. You're right. Let's head to the transport station, so we can leave here. There's nothing left here for us."

Jamie stood. The two girls locked arms and walked. There was already a line forming at the transport station. The girls walked up to the ticket window and showed their identification. They were immediately escorted to a large sterile looking room. Upon entering the doorway, a gush of air, which smelled like decaying flowers, blasted them. A male voice blared overhead, "Nothing to be concerned about. The air surge is a purifier to eliminate any contamination found on your clothing or hair. Take a seat. Momentarily, you will be guided to the loading tube."

Jamie turned toward Megan, but before she could say anything, Megan put her finger over her lips, motioning Jamie to be quiet. They took seats in the first row and waited. The windowless room with barren walls was a stark reminder they were leaving everything behind. Time seemed to stand still here. Jamie leaned into Megan's shoulder and drifted off to sleep. Jamie was jarred awake when a calming female voice came through the overhead speakers.

"Please proceed to the door directly in front of you. It will open. You need to step into the loading tube. Just stand still, the tube will carry you to the transport. Once the doors to the transport open, follow the lights on the floor. They will direct you to your seats. Make yourself comfortable in your seats. There's no reason to be alarmed when the shield lowers. You cannot leave the pod until we dock with the mother ship. However, you can talk, sleep, or eat on your trip."

Haltingly, the girls arose from their seats. It was then they noticed they were the only people in this waiting area. They grabbed one another's hand and ambled to the door. As soon as they stepped on the black mat in-front of the exit, it opened with a swish. The other side of the doorway revealed a bright white arched space. As quickly as they stepped through the doorway, they again heard the swish sound as the door closed behind them and the floor beneath them propelled them forward. They felt like they were rising uphill. The floor stopped moving and another set of double doors opened with a swoosh. The dimly lit space had small yellow lights on the floor forming a line. They started walking. Megan looked over her shoulder and noticed the lights behind them had disappeared. Only the lights leading the way remained. The lights curved around several corners and then ended at an opening where two reclining chairs were located. Besides the chairs, the space held a short table and a narrow portal on the wall. They looked at each other.

Megan said, "I believe this is where we are supposed to be."

"If you say so," said Jamie.

They stepped through the opening and immediately a lid descended from the ceiling, enclosing the opening and the space they occupied. The area was ample enough for them to move about, but provided no escape. Megan pulled back the covering over the window and peered into the darkness. She could barely see the earth below. The sun was growing even more dimly and the black smoke filled the air. The transport shook. They heard a faint whir, like an electric fan, then they felt themselves moving. Both girls stared out the window as the earth got smaller and smaller. Suddenly, the earth was exchanged with an explosion of fire, which filled the sky.

Megan dropped into her chair. "I think it was a good idea we left on this transport. Everything we knew is gone."

Jamie just shook her head in agreement as tears ran down her cheeks.

The Empty Chair

It's dark and so quiet. I'm grateful I still can recall happier times. My first memories revolve around being brought home to sit in the farmhouse kitchen. The woman would frequently hum as she worked, rattling pots and pans. Wafts of meats and vegetables cooking would fill the room. The temperature would rise; suddenly the doors would spring open, bringing men and boys filing into the room after working the fields. Talk would be loud. As quickly as they entered the kitchen, they would leave. The sounds of clean up differed from the meal preparation. Then the woman would be gone. I'd hear her throughout the afternoon, but if she wasn't cooking or cleaning, she wasn't in my presence.

Life in the house changed. It became much noisier and more individuals passed through the house. I learned two little girls joined the family. While they grew, one at a time would use me for a seat. A large white cloth would tie one girl in the chair. Then someone would sit in another chair and feed the one sitting on me. One at a time, they sat on me. I was the feeding chair until they were big enough to sit on a regular chair. As they grew, they would race around the table and fight over who would sit on me. Eventually they outgrew me, and the family moved to a different house in town. They moved me into the pantry room of the new house. I could still hear the woman talking with her girls. Her voice was like music, like water flowing over small rocks in a brook. People felt safe in her kitchen, which was vibrant. Her hair became white as snow and she moved slower. I felt safe and content in her presence.

Those two girls grew and left home. Many days, the house was quiet. During the day, the woman would leave. Weekends were different. The girls, now women, would return to the house with their men. After enjoying their meal, the women ended up in the kitchen chatting and cleaning up. I enjoyed hearing those voices in the house again. I was brought to the kitchen to be a feeding chair when another young person entered the house. This happened many times until they added five children to the family. I was happy to be part of the family again. As these children grew, someone would eventually place me back in the pantry room. The cycles of the house becoming quiet seem to happen more frequently. Then gradually one of these children would grow, bring someone home and eventually they would bring a little one into the house. This happened six more times before the house became painfully quiet. The silence was scary. I missed the music of her voice, the thrill of little feet running around the house. I hated feeling so alone.

After more days than I can count, the two daughters returned to the house. I had hated being alone in the quiet and dark. They sounded so sad. I heard them talk of a sale. They took some items from the house. The girls left, locking the door again. The silence was deafening. I was cold in the house, and so scared. I couldn't understand what this meant.

The daughters returned to the house a few days later with several men. Those men carried objects outside. They took me out and set me on the cold ground. The sky was grey; the wind swirled around me. Crowds arrived and walked around peering at all the items setting on the ground with me. Slowly, I realized those other items probably belonged to the lady I loved. Suddenly a man was picking up items and talking rapidly. I couldn't understand him, but I watched in amazement. Then I was lifted. The man rattled some words and people started shouting numbers. I watched as one sister stood behind the others. One would raise their card or shout a number; then the other would do the same. Eventually, the shouting stopped, and I was handed to the sister standing in the front. She was thrilled, and I went home with her. There I took up residence in her kitchen. It was a room often filled with good fragrances. Laughter often filled the space. Seldom did children sit upon me, but the woman generally placed her handbag on me. I felt loved and valued. Hers was a fun house and reminded me of the older woman's house, even though there weren't children sitting on me. I missed the older woman less when I was in this home. Then this place became too quiet. The woman was seldom in the kitchen. Silence filled the space. Deep feelings of sadness filled me, as I didn't know what would happen. I remembered those cold, lonely days. I sat, an empty chair in the corner, scared about what would happen to me. I didn't know if anyone would take me home and allow me to feel loved and happy again. How long will I be able to keep these memories?

Ho, Ho, Ho!

The stockings are all hung on the mantel with care.

Not with hopes of gifts, but stuffed full of memories from Christmases past.

Ho, Ho, Ho! Santa should come on a sleigh.

Ha, ha, ha—no snow here, but then there are no children here either. So perhaps no one will notice.

The music of the season fills the airwaves, the shopping spaces, vehicles and homes. Taking listeners on journeys back to their past, those years of prior Christmases. Some smile, some shake their head and think it is all nonsense. I'm one who smiles with memories of being a child, memories of being a mom and surprising a child. My memories overflow and allow me to derive pleasure from watching others as they celebrate the season.

Back home, it is quiet here. Not an eerie quietness, but a quietness which settles like a soft comforter one wants to snuggle into. This season has brought contentment, joy and peace. I revel in these feelings.

Lights and baubles bedazzle the tree; some shiny and some not.

Each bauble holds the secret of its history, waiting for the dark when only the lights of the tree allow them to speak of their origins and how they became part of this holiday tradition. How I would enjoy hearing them tell their own story, how they feel being out of the box for a brief season.

The nativity pieces on full display sit in several rooms, emitting their own scenes and memories from years past within the family tree. Now they live together in our home, with our family, and share their pride of being treasured for so many years. Their story continues to live in our lives.

Ho, Ho, Ho!

May this Christmas season come to your home bringing hope for the future, eyes to see the good in others, and peace to all who enter through your doorway, thus leaving you with many happy memories.

True Home

They learned I had arrived
and said welcome home.
How those words warmed my heart.
It's been two years since last we met.
Yet weekly we've joined on screen
where stories and friendship are shared.

Me…
A body locked in geographical space and time.
Neither yet both…
at home here or there.
Each location is magical and calls to me.
I desire both
yet physical limitations constrain me to one.

Perhaps never have I been completely at home
anywhere,
which may contribute to the peace of knowing
heaven which knows no bounds
will be my final resting place.

Message and the Bottle

Tasha trudged up the steps and unlocked the front door. She hadn't visited this house in years. The last falling out with her father was her breaking point. It happened after her mother died. She went to visit her dad. He was a hard man who showed few emotions. He knew judgement, criticism and anger; all of these he threw on her the day she visited. She stormed out the door, letting it slam shut behind her, determined she would *never* go back again.

And here she was. Today, climbing those steps, putting the key in the entrance lock again and entering the house. It was different. The house was like a pharaoh's tomb. The king was dead, yet all his belongings were stashed away here. It had become her responsibility to deal with all of this stuff. She plodded down the hallway, peering first into one room and then the next. The place was full of stuff. Where to start?

The kitchen might be the easiest, with the fewest emotional pulls. She decided not. It was the room she had spent the most time with her dear mother. No, the kitchen must wait. She approached the doorway to the cellar and considered looking down there. Down the stairs she went. Using the switch at the bottom of the steps, she turned on the main light. The space lit up. It was just one large space with no dividing walls. Different areas had been relegated to different purposes. Other than a few nooks and crannies, everything was visible.

Tasha decided to begin here. She returned to her vehicle to retrieve packing boxes and a notebook. Entering the house this time didn't feel so ominous. She had a plan.

The laundry area was surveyed. Nothing there to remove, so the items were written on a list. Her father's work area was next. Everything was orderly. After Tasha filled a small toolbox with items she considered might be useful at her house, an inventory of the remaining tools was added to the list. She sighed. *This is going better than I expected.*

There was camping gear in one corner. Christmas ornaments, her father's military footlocker, and a few of her old toys laid in another area. Decisions were made regarding disposition. This goes with the house, toss, keep, or put in the sale. It was obvious she would have to sort many boxes before final decisions were established. Another pile was created—for later.

She entered the space behind the steps and gasped. What had once been her mother's overflow pantry area had become a wine/liquor storage area. She pulled the chain to bring light in this space.

When did her father acquire this? She knew he enjoyed an occasional drink after dinner, but what did he plan for this trove of liquor? Tasha knew little about liquor and stared at the bottles in amazement. Through the dim light, she saw a storage shelf. It appeared to hold a collection of old bottles. As she reached for one of the dusty, grimy bottles, she wondered, *How long has he been amassing this collection? What will I do with these?*

To her amazement, there was a pamphlet attached to the neck of this bottle. She looked at the writing and saw "A Legend of Lost Liquor." Then she put the bottle in a box she planned to take with her. *I'll read this later.* The liquor decisions would have to wait. She had other things to decide.

Returning upstairs, she set the box on the kitchen table and started sorting out the bathroom. This was easier. Many of the items she'd take to the men's shelter. The rest would go in the garbage. She pulled a few towels out to use as rags at her house. She looked at the clock. *I should have started here. I might have gotten another room done. Then I would have felt like I accomplished something today.*

Tasha snatched her purse and the box with the liquor bottle from the table, locked up the house, and drove away. Once home, she set those same items on her kitchen table and ran upstairs to change for dinner. She raced back downstairs when the doorbell rang. Mark was standing there with three yellow roses in his hand. He came inside and they quickly exchanged kisses.

"I'll put these in water for you. Why don't you finish getting ready? We have reservations in town tonight."

"Sounds great. They are beautiful. Thank you. I'll be down in a minute."

When Tasha came back downstairs, Mark was in the dining room examining the liquor bottle she had brought back from her father's house. The roses were laid on the table.

"This is amazing. Have you read the pamphlet? ...and where did you get this?"

"Wait. No, I haven't read the pamphlet. Remember, I went to my dad's to clean out the house today. I found a stash of liquor in the basement. There were many bottles like this. I brought one home to research what it is. I can't understand why dad had so much liquor."

"Let's go to dinner and talk about it there."

The hostess seated them at a quiet table. Mark ordered a bottle of wine without asking what Tasha might like. She was tired and wanted to relax, but thought it was out of character for Mark to not ask what her preference was. He seemed so preoccupied.

"What's this all about? You seem so serious."

"Do you have any idea what you've found?"

The excitement in his voice was building.

"No, what are we talking about?"

"The liquor you found. That bottle is ancient, and rare. The liquor is older than your father."

"What would he be doing with it?"

"My guess is he purchased it while in the military."

"So, what do you know about this?"

"According to the pamphlet, the liquor is rumored, or as legend says, to be tied to the renown Afrika Korps of Field Marshal Erwin Rommel. They found a vast wine and spirit cellar during their raids crossing North Africa. They turned up over a million liters of top quality liquor—Scotch whiskey, Jamaican rum, London gin, and French cognac. All was stored in huge oak casks. This was early in World War 2. Of course, he shared some with his troops, or perhaps they insisted he share and the rest of the alcohol was shipped to the Italian village of Nettuno, Italy, where it was to be warehoused. The war continued to rage. On January 22, 1944, the United States VI Corps, including the 3rd US Infantry Division of the Fifth Army, assaulted the beach at Anzio. One of the objectives was the village of Nettuno. There they captured a unique war trophy of some 250,000 gallons of the best quality booze. Eventually, the Delva Distillery was commissioned to bottle the liquor captured at Nettuno. Lit. P. Casseti

Company of Rome created the extravagantly formatted labels."

Tasha had her arms on the table and was sitting on the edge of her seat. She did not know what she had discovered, but the story was fascinating. *How does this relate to my father?*

She said, "How to do you know all this?"

"Tasha, I've been trying to tell you, you have a treasure here. I want you to understand it and then you have to decide what you'll do with it. I've gotten most of the info from the pamphlet and some from history I remember reading."

The waiter brought their wine to the table, poured each of them a glass, and Mark ordered dinner for them.

"Sit back, enjoy your wine, and I'll finish the story."

"Yes, please. Tell me more."

"Some General for the Allied Forces, Italy, became the holder in escrow for the liquor. We'll get his name from the pamphlet later. All the bottles were labeled and packed into wooden cases. A long since forgotten Allied Military Government unit bearing the initials R.A.A.C. marked a special label on each bottle, which testified chemical tests had assured compliance with Allied military purity standards. After the May 1945 Allied victory, American troops were stationed as part of the occupation task. Some senior officers and high-ranking military personnel were transferred from Italy to occupation duty in Austria."

"They probably enjoyed some of this liquor as well," said Tasha.

"There's no record or information regarding how or why, but before the end of 1945, a train carrying all the remaining stock of Afrika Korps liquor arrived in Linz,

Austria. There were over half a million liters. All the bottles were carefully laid down, with each layer insulated in a bed of straw, deep within the central city wine caves. Periodically, selected quantities were withdrawn for official US Military Government entertainment.

In 1947, the remaining several hundred thousand bottles in the city were transferred away from the Allied occupation forces. The Linz national customs office of the new Austrian Republic became the new curator.

There's no record of the liquors again until 1976, when some senior business executives representing the legal owners of the remaining supply approached the U.S. Army with an offer to sell specific amounts of the liquor for resale.

They stocked the liquors in Class VI stores on bases within Europe, where they quickly sold out.

"Your father must have purchased the wine when he was stationed overseas."

"Yeah. He must have."

"Hey Tasha, what's going on? Suddenly, you seem so far away."

"I'm trying to put bits and pieces of conversations together. My brain is cluttered with thoughts of things Dad said and then finding the liquor downstairs."

"Anything I can help with?"

"Not sure. Maybe you can help me find someone to assist with selling all the liquor. But I realize I have to rethink what emptying dad's house means. I need to rethink what this process will involve. Let's enjoy dinner and explore the topic later."

The following days turned into weeks, which turned into months. Tasha found renewed significance in sorting through the things in her father's house. Items she had once considered inconceivable one would keep took on new meaning as she uncovered history and hidden value. Still being a minimalist at heart, she enlisted Mark's help in finding those specializing in her dad's various collectables and watched as the items sold and the cash grew. Occasionally, she'd find something of interest to her and take it home. The estate attorney was handling the paperwork, so she only had to meet with this lady periodically to sign papers. Dad's house was getting emptied and in the process Tasha was gaining a different understanding of who her father had been.

Mark was present when she met with an agent to go through the house.

"This place looks so much different. You've put a lot of work into this house. Are you sure you want to sell it?" said Mark.

Tasha hesitated. She glanced around the space and looked out the window.

The agent quickly said, "Your house is in a great neighborhood. It's quiet and within walking distance of some excellent schools. You should take advantage of this excellent market. This house won't last long."

Tasha said, "I'm not sure what to do. Thank you for giving me an idea of what the house is worth. I need to consider what I want. I'll be in touch."

The agent smiled at Tasha. "I understand times like this create many emotions and memories. You take your time and call me when you're ready."

"Thank you."

Tasha hadn't decided what she would do. But she knew she was no longer angry when she entered the house.

Lake Memories

I stand on the deck watching the sunset fill the sky with radiant colors of red, orange, and yellow reaching higher and higher into the heavens. Vermillion being reflected back into the water. The colors seem endless. The silhouette of our sailboat swaying on the waves as they gently roll onto the shore and the quiet of evening settles on the land and within my body. Boats tied at piers do not create such striking silhouettes against the evening colors. After an intense day in the office, I retreat to this location; there are no demands here and I can escape toxic personalities. Here I slip into the peace and solitude of the atmosphere. It's quiet on the deck. The evening crickets have not yet appeared and the waterfowl have retired. I could get lost in this atmosphere. Of course, the pesky mosquitoes are swarming this evening, just like any other day, and they ultimately chase me inside. The lit candles on the table are ineffective in driving them away. The mosquitoes and humidity mar my tranquil moment. After extinguishing the candles, I return to the house where dinner is waiting to be served.

Saturday morning arrives. I've been cleaning the bedroom and have the patio doors open to allow the morning breeze to waft into the room. I stop and lean against the doorframe, savoring the beauty of the morning sky. It's early enough the sky is still blue. The pelicans circling above slowly descend to light on the water. It's my pleasure to stand there and just observe them. I become mesmerized watching them glide on the water. They are so regal, bright white against the dark aqua water, with the sun glinting against the ripples, creating pockets of sparkle. Stunning yet peaceful are the descriptors for this scene. This is the memory I return to when I wish to relax or need to reduce my blood pressure.

Winter arrives, and so do our short-term seasonal neighbors. They've hauled their pickup trucks filled with fishing gear out onto the lake. The whooping and hollering punctuates the cold air as they haul in their daily catch, build bonfires on the ice and allow their kids to play winter games. I'm happy to enjoy their joy from the warmth of my home. Their tenure is short. They move their equipment on and are gone before the ice thins and spring thaws begin.

Winter storms created another unique Icelandic wonder on our shoreline. The winds blow across the miles of water and create ice shoves, which display sheets of ice standing on edge against the rip rap at the water's edge. The more magnificent displays would then last for several days. After trekking through the snow and descending the three terraces, you can behold them. There we marvel at the creative work of the forceful winter wind.

We still laugh at the incident, which became a memory. It was late in the season. We recognized it was too late to be on the water, but we craved one last sail. Throwing caution to the wind, off we sailed. Tom swung the tiller to come about, but realized he hadn't alerted me to his intentions. He turned and responded quickly as he witnessed me being swept off the trampoline by the main sail boom. His quick reaction allowed him to grab my ankle before I was fully overboard. There I was, bobbing behind the Hobie, with him grasping my ankle. Thankfully, my core strength was strong enough to allow me to work my way back onto the trampoline. What followed was a frigid sail back home. We discussed how the day could have gone differently. I had my life preserver on. It was late in the season and the water was cold. The neighbors had previously pulled their boats from the water. So none were out this day. Watercraft powered by sails have limited maneuverability. In the months to follow, we were in the office one evening when I casually inquired about the possibility of acquiring a boat we could sit IN, versus the Hobie which we sat ON. Tom told me I was such a good sport being willing to continue sailing. He quickly began research for a larger sailboat. We sold the Hobie, to acquire an old 26-foot MacGregor, which we enjoyed until we moved from the lake.

The lake itself is huge, encompassing 10,500 acres once home to the Blackhawk Indians where they hunted and grew wild rice. The rice is long gone and the natural dams, since replaced with structured dams, allowed the water levels to become manageable on a year-round basis. Three large bird hunting properties are located around the lake, an area which is renowned for duck hunting. It's a large lake, but not deep. These properties and lake conditions create unique situations in this area. Few lakes have so few waterfront homes. And there are fewer weekend boaters on the water than other large water bodies in Wisconsin. In the summer months, the weekend boaters who arrived, often zipped around with water skiers in tow. Year-round fishermen trolled the water in their small craft. In warm weather, party barges appeared on the weekends and anchor on one of the sand bars. There they remained for the day, whooping and splashing in the shallow water. We used our ski boat for company or when we went to dinner at one of several restaurants on the lake, as this was quicker than driving around the lake.

Not all memories of the lake invoke tranquility.

I find it interesting to ponder how we choose what memories to retain, how we frame them and then how they shape us. Living there was special. When we left, it was clear we were moving on to something different. The mountains called us, yet the memories linger.

Chariot Drivers

White horses whipped to a frenzy by the chariot drivers
stir up a storm behind
pulling the dark mass to follow them.
Below
this tumult bends the fronds close to the ground.
Palm trunks sway back and forth
while their branches all flay in one direction.
Awakening what in the underworld?
Above hints of blue and light remain
with few penetrating the dark mass.

Once these chariots pass
white swirls remain against the blue.
Large spots of light again kiss the ground.
The fronds gently sway as the palms again stand erect
and tall.
White snowdrops scattered against the green
display their finery.
Eagerly
they greet the arrival of regal daffodils.
All indications are of something better
than what the chariot drivers bring.
How long will we enjoy the signs of life?
Or are we doomed to the spirits of those savage
chariots?

The Tourist

Many aspects of my flight home were different from previous travels. We'd been gone for two months. Traveling during Covid uncertainties made advance planning impossible. The war in Ukraine added to the tensions. This flight didn't pull up to the gate. Instead, we took a bus to the tarmac, where we boarded the plane. On the bus ride, I sat next to a gentleman from Switzerland. He and his wife purchased last minute tickets to San Diego because they felt Ukraine was too close for comfort. They planned to sit out the war at their home in Palm Desert.

I sensed the tension caused by the conflict. Many people connected to people caught in the conflict were my acquaintances. My heart was heavy and hurt for all the people impacted by the invasion. The emotional toll this event would have on individuals was hard to comprehend.

I was grateful we found our seats and stowed our carry-on luggage with no problem. My husband pulled out his headsets and reading material. Me, a publication to read if I couldn't sleep.

He strode down the right aisle of the plane, looking for his seat. There it was. Tall and lanky, he easily tossed his duffle bag into the overhead storage bin and took his seat. He couldn't seem to get settled. A woman approached him.

"Excuse me, I believe you're in my seat."

After a brief exchange, he realized he was one row off. He moved into the seat next to me. I noticed how jumpy his actions were. He kept looking around and behind him, and his legs were constantly jiggling. I considered he was nervous about flying and would quiet down after the plane was airborne. His actions didn't meet my expectations. He continued to glance around and kept bouncing his legs. It seemed like his hands were constantly moving as well. He finally pulled out his tablet, which seemed to settle him for a few minutes.

I made a mental note that he was wearing a pair of jeans, a printed t-shirt and tennis shoes. His face was long, his chin length mousy brown hair was straight and very fine. He, like everyone else on the flight, donned a face-mask so other features were hidden. I figured he was in his early thirties.

He saw my husband looking for the headphone jack connection point.

"The outlet is on the armrest."

"Thank you."

With this quick exchange, my husband was plugged in for most of the flight. I'm not sure he even noticed how unsettled this guy was.

Flight attendants arrived, serving drinks. I had never seen more of him. His nose was long, with a marked hook. We exchanged a few pleasantries.

I asked, "What is your final destination after San Diego?"

"Oh, I'm getting off at San Diego."

His eyes sparkled.

"This is my first trip to America. I can't wait. Oh, I've been on other trips, but not to America."

His eyes sparkled and his hands moved with rapid excitement.

"I can't wait to arrive in American and absorb as much culture as possible."

"How long will you be there?"

"Oh, I'm going to work on a yacht moored at Imperial Beach, needing some repairs. I'm scheduled to be there for ten days. I hope to stay at least that long. And while I'm there, I want to experience all the American Fast Food."

I laughed, then apologized.

"We have more than fast food. What do you want to try?"

"Churches Chicken, and some burger joint."

"Let me suggest In & Out Burgers. My daughter thinks it is the best."

Masks back on, we each settled back into our reading. Me, my publication, him, his tablet.

He appeared to settle down a little more, and I relaxed, releasing the thoughts he might potentially be a threat to flight safety. We shared several other brief conversations during meals, then again would each settle back to relax as the hours rolled by. During each of those conversation times, I was struck by his uncontrollable excitement at this transatlantic flight taking him to America, a location he's longed to visit.

Settling back into my chair, my thoughts drifted to my first transatlantic flight, which was actually my first experience with air travel. My excitement back than probably paralleled his. How much has changed since those days! The increased security measures, reduction in space and flight amenities have reduced air travel to a way to get from one location to another. My husband prefers to sit by the isle, and I prefer to sit by him so window seats are mostly part of my past. My excitement is limited to where I'm going, the people I will meet there, and what I'll experience once I arrive. The flight is merely a means to the end these days.

Before departing the plane, we spoke again.

"I wish you the best during your trip to California. I hope you experience as many things as you hope. Thank you for sharing your excitement with me. It reminded me of how flying used to be for me. I appreciate that."

"Thank you."

"I'd like to suggest you keep in mind, America is big and culture is distinctive in different regions of the country. Try to return and experience another area.

"Thank you. I hope too. Safe travels home."

We completed a long flight. Our bags reclaimed, a quick pass through customs, and our ride home was waiting for us.

Memories of the emotions evoked by someone else's excitement reminded me to not take for granted the gifts of each day.

Shooting Stars

Life goals
My guiding stars
Live with integrity
Make a difference in other's lives

Shooting Stars

People enter
Some stay
Others drift away
Some have blessed me
They share my impact on them
Some depart with nary a word

Colorado introduced me to shooting stars
What a sight
Against the velvet navy of night
A bright white light appears
Shooting across the sky
Before vanishing into the darkness
Leaving me to question if what I saw was real
Had I blinked
I would have missed the sight

Now
Learning to be alert
I enjoy the night sky
In a different way

Beauty fills the skies
Stars still fascinate me
Yet those bright streaking flashes
Stun and remind me
How fleeting life is
For each of us
We may impact others around us
But only if they are looking
And catch our brief shine in the arc of time
It matters little if they see or not
But that we continue on our trajectory
We must follow our calling

Why Eleven

Family heirlooms are being disbursed as my aunt's house is being readied for sale. A relative was talking with me about some of the antique dishes in my aunt's china cabinet, which were passed down from my grandmother. She noted there were only eleven long stemmed pink wine goblets. I laughed. Oh, there's a story there.

My grandmother, Dorothy, known by her grandchildren as Granny, shared the following story with me many times.

I often stood in front of her china cabinet, enjoying the many beautiful things on display within. The china was white, had two thin silver bands with a delicate blue floral pattern between the bands. We used the china for family dinners hosted weekly in the dining room, or at other large gatherings. Other pieces of porcelain were also on display there. Many had specific purposes.

I knew Granny had worked as a live-in maid, or house servant, for a wealthy family in town during her late teen years. She was proud of the fact she saved money and purchased her china and other household items prior to her wedding.

Because the beauty of those pink etched wine glasses fascinated me, I asked Granny why they were never used. She shared the following story.

She and my grandfather, Victor, were married. Granny stated the first time she used those glasses, my grandfather knocked one over and it broke. She felt he was clumsy around delicate objects, and she wanted no more of her glasses to break.

So they sat on the shelf.

As I ponder those memories, I find it odd for Granny to have made such a statement about my grandfather, as she rarely had harsh words towards another. It was such a disappointment to her that one had broken. Because I moved often and enjoyed scoping out antique stores, I would scour the shops hoping to find a pink stemmed wine glass to complete her set. I hoped finding the twelfth would make her happy. My efforts were fruitless, but I enjoyed the quest.

I always knew someday my aunt would inherit those glasses.

It seems no one else in the family knew this story, as I was the one to peer into Granny's china cabinet. My fascination with dishes and glassware continued on for many years. There was a silent lesson in this experience for me.

I desired for those close to me to share in appreciating the detail, or beauty in china or handmade pottery, and used my dishes. Thus, allowing family memories to be made while sharing meals together in the hopes someone in the family may want some pieces I have collected. Yes, sometimes a piece gets chipped or broken. The responsible person usually feels guilty and apologizes. I assure them, I know it wasn't intentional; but most importantly, we were enjoying them together, and the piece was part of the memory.

So, to the recipient of the eleven beautiful, pink, etched, stemmed, wine glasses, may you have many years of enjoying the use of them. It's my hope the family tradition of appreciating lovely dinnerware continues in your family and you remember, such was the gift from Dorothy. You now know why there are eleven.

The Attic

Sasha watched her mother descend the ladder, balancing the box in one hand. After setting the box on the floor, she returned to the attic twice more to retrieve additional boxes. Sasha had seen no one ever enter the attic. It was a strange space only accessible through the garage, using a ladder. Mabel carried the boxes into the dining room and sorted the contents.

"Ugh! Why must I go through all this?"

"Just leave it, if you don't want to go through it?" said Sasha.

Mabel snuffled.

"You know I can't do that. Your father wouldn't return anything of mine if it was in these boxes."

"I hope you're not at this too long. I have to run."

Sasha left, still thinking about her mother sitting there. Their divorce had been long and ugly. The process was almost complete, but Mabel was disappointed the courts had not awarded her more. Mabel had two months to leave the house. Sasha had an apartment in town and was certain her mom would be okay. After the divorce, the mother and daughter believed life would return to normal. Sasha planned to check in on her mother in a couple of days.

When Sasha returned to her childhood home, she felt like a stranger. Boxes were everywhere. Mabel had been busy packing the things she was taking from the house. The boxes from the attic were gone. In their place was one box and it had Sasha's name written on the top. Sasha went looking for her mom and found her packing things in the bathroom.

"I thought you had two months to leave the house."

"I do. However, I think I'll be happier once I'm gone from here. Your father slowly cruises the street every night. Sometimes he even parks across the street."

"Yuk," said Sasha.

"It makes me feel uncomfortable. I have an apartment and plan to move in before the weekend."

"Are you alright, mom?"

"Sure. I'll be fine, honey. I just need to move on. There's a box on the table for you. Did you find it?"

"Yes, what's in it?"

"Remember the boxes from the attic?"

"Uh, huh."

"Well, those are some family history papers. They're from your father's side of the family, and I don't want them. I thought you might be interested in them."

"I'll take a look. Aren't you going to leave them for dad?"

"No. He had an extensive list of everything he expected to be here when he takes possession of the house. Those things weren't on the list. He'll never miss them. Take the box and sort it out at your convenience."

Sasha and Mabel went out for dinner, taking Sasha's car. Arriving back at the house, Sasha pulled in the drive-way behind Mabel's car.

"Hey mom, I didn't notice you have a flat tire when we left."

"I'll have to call Triple-A again in the morning."

"What do you mean, again?"

"Oh, this has been happening several nights each week. I'll awake in the morning to find I have flat tires. The authorities say it is only mischievous as the tires aren't damaged. The valve cap had been removed. No actual damage, but incredibly frustrating and inconvenient."

"Dad?"

"I can only guess it's him. I don't stay up looking out the windows. I'm hopeful this will stop once I move and he has the house again."

"Do you want me to stay this evening?"

"No. Don't be silly. I'll be fine."

"Ok. I'll wait here until you are in the house and are confident you are alone. Come back, turn on the porch light and wave to me. If you don't come back, I'm calling the police and coming in."

"Sasha, don't be silly. I'll be fine."

"Mom…"

"Ok, honey. I will return to the porch to let you know everything is fine. Thanks for a great evening out tonight."

"Night. Love you, mom."

Sasha knew her father was a man who had strong opinions and didn't tolerate others questioning his authority. She knew he was angry about the divorce and intended for Mabel to regret her decision to be free of him. Yet she grappled with the thought he would stalk her mom and vandalize her vehicle. Sasha knew these truths, even though she tried to forget them, just as she tried to forget the day her father called her at work.

"Sasha, I need you to come to court tomorrow to testify on my behalf at the divorce hearing," said Ted.

Stammering, Sasha said, "You want what? I can't do that. You're my dad, and she's my mom. I'm unwilling to take sides."

Ted persisted, and Sasha declined, repeating what she'd previously said. Ted's temper flared.

"Girl, you'll live to regret this decision."

Then he slammed the phone down. Sasha sat at her desk, shaking, still holding the phone. She looked around the office, put the phone down, and gathered up her belongings. Stopping at her manager's desk, she asked if she could leave for the day, as she didn't feel well. She kept replaying the conversation in her mind. The incident left her frustrated, shaken and angry. *How could a parent expect a child to take sides in an adult conflict? Ok, so she wasn't actually a child anymore, but she would always be their child.*

She never mentioned the incident to her mother. Similarly, Mabel never spoke of the evening she was out for dinner with a male friend and Ted arrived at the restaurant. He swaggered over to their table and whipped a gun out. Waving it around in front of their faces, he threatened he could blow them to bits. They sat in their seats, frozen until he left.

Neither mother nor daughter wanted to frighten the other, so they kept these truths hidden, just like neither wanted to admit just how angry, controlling, abusive, and mentally unstable Ted was.

Heatwave

Survived today
Setting sun brought
Ocean breezes inland

Quiet late dinner
At end of day's activity

Iced wine swirling
In long stemmed glass
Rests on table
While I recline
Under patio lights
Pondering familiar news
Of the day

Grandchildren
Many
Present reasons to be
On my knees
No easy answers

A resilient crowd
They are
Strong
Self-reliant
They walk into their
Uncertain futures

I watch
Offer what encouragement
I can
Knowing I have
No answers tonight

Knowing with tomorrow
Returns the sweltering heat
And unresolved issues

Tonight the crickets sing
Reminding me
Winter's coming
Their song settles my mind
Jasmine wafts
Through the air
Stars sparkle overhead
Against the navy sky

Tonight
All is well

Goodbye / Hello

2020 – I join with friends around the globe to say Adieu
Your stories will be told for years to come
No need for more
…and now I direct my gaze forward

2021 – enter
Open our eyes to see fresh things
Teach us to see beauty in the little as well as the grand
Remind us there is nothing new under the sun
And that peace comes through faith
Let such faith grow in our lives
As we recognize all of mankind is suffering
We make a difference one step at a time
Give us courage to take those individual steps

Welcome 2021
The world is ready for a change
How about you?

Best wishes to all in this new year

Jilted

The door of the courthouse burst open and Rose came flying through the opening. Her blouse was askew, her trench coat was thrown over one arm, and her briefcase was in the other hand. The wind blew her long hair back. At the top of the steps, she paused, took a deep breath, and carefully descended. Her high heels left her a little unstable. She glanced back over her shoulder and slowly descended the steps.

When she reached the bottom, she surveyed the area to find a bench. She spotted one by the fountain and headed in that direction. The sound of children playing in the nearby park filled the air and her mind as she slumped onto the bench. Her briefcase fell to the ground as tears streamed down her face.

Rose sat there sobbing for some time. She never saw Rob exit the building. He strutted down the steps. As he reached the bottom, he stopped for a moment and looked around. He observed Rose sitting on the park bench and considered walking over to talk with her, but didn't know what he might say to ease her pain. It was over! He wanted it to be over. Before he could consider that idea any further, Theresa came rushing around the corner and threw herself into his arms.

"Is it over? Are you finally finished with her? Let's go celebrate." said Theresa.

Some of his bravado seemed to diminish as he looked at Theresa and then glanced toward Rose. "We started the process. I didn't expect it to be so rough on Rose. I really never intended to hurt her."

"What do you mean, you started the process? Today was supposed to be the end of the process."

"Rose is pregnant, and the judge won't finalize anything until the baby is born and we have a paternity test to determine if I'm the father. All the settlement agreements may change."

"What? This just isn't possible. You informed me you were done with her and wanted us to get on with our lives. The baby can't be yours. What is going on here?"

"Theresa, I'm tired. Today was far more stressful than I anticipated, can't you understand that?"

"What I know is you informed me after today, we wouldn't have to sneak around anymore and could plan our future. I've made reservations for us in the city to celebrate. What are we supposed to do now? I propose we continue with our plans and accept this as a minor detour, not the end of things."

"Maybe... I don't know."

"Come on. Let's not waste a good reservation."

Rob reluctantly took Theresa's hand and threw one more glance toward Rose, as the two of them turned and walked down the street. The days turned into weeks, and the weeks rolled into months. News of Rob and Rose's pending divorce was common knowledge, so there was no longer a need for Theresa and Rob to remain discrete about their relationship. Theresa was relentless about wanting to plan their future; buy a house; go shopping for furniture; make travel plans while Rob was meeting with his attorney and learning the realities of his financial responsibilities if the child was his. He didn't know how to tell Theresa his resources may no longer provide the lifestyle they had been talking about. He considered himself a clod for leading her on, but didn't wish to lose her if the child was not his.

Theresa had located a house near the country club and wanted Rob to make an offer to purchase. Rob kept making excuses until the day the realtor called him at work. He knew he couldn't afford property in the country-club neighborhood. That afternoon, he left work early and went to Theresa's apartment, where he packed up his things before she arrived home.

He placed a single rose on the table with a note. "Thanks for the memories. You deserve better. I just can't do this." Then he placed the apartment key next to the rose, turned, picked up his luggage, and walked out the door. He had already reserved a stay at one of the local hotels for a couple of weeks, stopped and purchased a six-pack of beer, then headed to his room. He blocked Theresa's number on his phone before deleting her contact information. Tomorrow he would tell his secretary to not accept any calls from her.

Rose was sleeping in her hospital room, surrounded by her parents and her sister. Her dad looked up when the door slowly opened. Everyone gasped when they saw Rob sheepishly standing in the doorway. Rose's father jumped out of his chair and headed to the doorway.

"It's not appropriate for you to be here."

"I… I just needed to see Rose, to make sure she's okay, and tell her how beautiful the baby is," said Rob.

"I'll make sure she gets the message when she wakes up. You need to leave before you create a scene."

Rob didn't know how to deal with his father-in-law's firm stance, so he shrugged and turned around.

Rob returned to his apartment, where he spent many evenings pondering the legal implications and how this divorce would be settled. With the baby born, the paternity test results would soon be available. His lawyer emphasized if the test results suggested he was the father, the court would require he make support payments to Rose for years. Medical expenses, schooling and other costs related to the child would be split between the two parents. This situation would necessitate he and Rose figure out how to work together. How's that going to happen when we don't even talk? He recognized he was going to have to reason with Rose.

Rob let Rose get home and be settled with the baby. He pulled into the parking lot and hoped her parents weren't staying with her. As he exited his car, he surveyed the lot. He saw Rose's vehicle parked, but not her parent's car so he headed into the building and rang the buzzer for Rose's apartment. He inhaled a deep breath and tried to smile as he stood in front of her door, not knowing what to expect.

Rose opened the door, but stood in the doorway with one hand on the door. She appeared tired, yet looked stunning. Rob had forgotten how beautiful she was.

She looked at him and said, "Yes?"

"Rose, I… I thought we should talk. Can I come in for a few minutes? I won't stay long."

Rose looked around, shrugged, then said, "I guess, for a few minutes. I'd like you to leave before Tabatha wakes up."

"Ok, sure."

She stepped aside, and Rob stepped into the apartment.

"Wow. Your place is lovely."

"Thank you. We can talk in the den," she said as she entered the room and settled herself in the rocking chair.

Rob took a seat on the couch.

He looked at her for a moment and said, "You know we're going to court again soon. If Tabatha is mine, things are going to get very complicated."

"If she's yours? Hmph… There won't be any question about who's child she is, but we can save that discussion for another day. Things are already complicated. What are you proposing?"

"Rose, I'm willing to disregard the whole paternity test results and consider Tabatha mine, if you'll take me back. Let's just forget about the divorce."

Rose appeared shocked, then she burst out in laughter. Between her hoots, she spit out the words, "No, way. You are too funny. I think it's time for you to leave."

Still laughing, she stood and headed toward the door.

"But, Rose. Honey. Can't we talk about this?"

Rose opened the door and held it open with her foot.

"We've said everything there is to be said today."

Rob stood and walked to the door. As he stepped through the doorway, he turned to look at Rose. She appeared sad as she shook her head and closed the door.

Rose fell against the door and thought, Men!

Coffee Time

This memory from my childhood takes me back to when many women stayed home; took care of domestic matters and raised the children. I remember a summer day where I slept later than usual. The smell of cinnamon wafting through the house awoke me. I jumped out of bed, ran down the hall, and peered into the kitchen. There she stood, at the counter, wearing an apron, arranging a vase of cut flowers. She always grew an amazing assortment of fresh flowers which encircled our garden. Often she would cut them and display vases throughout the house.

Immediately, I knew "the ladies" were coming today. The table was arranged with an embroidered tea cloth, good china, crystal glasses, and silver, all set and waiting for guests. As the coffee pot purred, it belched out the smell of coffee, which competed with the cinnamon fragrance already wafting in the air. The gathering of these ladies occurred several times a month, and always at our house. I ran to my sister's room to make sure she was up. She too, savored the delicious fragrances hanging in the air. We each dressed and concocted plans of things we could do to be around home during the day. Even at a young age, we recognized this activity as something special. Mom's mood would be joyful all day, and we coveted the sweet delicacies soon to come from the oven.

I found the days when "the ladies" visited to be an indulgence in many ways. Both were neighbors who were older than my mom. They treated my sister and me like we were someone special in their lives, remembering us at birthdays, holidays and even bringing small gifts to us when they returned from traveling. We excitedly shared what was happening in our lives and they sat like a captivated audience as we told our tales. We'd share conversation with them and each be offered a plate of treats and a glass of milk. Then we'd retreat with our snacks to the back porch and let them have their conversation. We didn't listen to their conversations, but occasionally the sound of their laughter would ring through the house. At some point one of them moved out of the neighborhood, but both my mother and I established a long-lasting relationship with the remaining neighbor; a retired English literature professor. My friendship was one which endured throughout her life. She and I shared common interests in books, travel, and cultures. She was the first person to encourage me to write.

Still not a coffee drinker, I look back at my mother's coffee time with these neighborhood friends, and recognize how her activity shaped aspects of who I am. As a child, I took their gatherings for granted and failed to realize how important her interactions with these women were. All her life, my mother maintained relationships with other women, many of them older than herself. She was an example to me. Female friendships are an important aspect of my life, as well.

For me, it's not coffee time, but tea time. A vast assortment of teas line my cupboard and one often fills a teapot ready for enjoyment. I'll go somewhere special to enjoy a pot of tea with a friend, or invite others to my home. I prepare the table and plan for the time to share with a friend. Over this hot brew in a peaceful environment, friendships have flourished. I've heard it's a dying art to entertain this way.

And now it falls to me. It's my pleasure to keep this tradition alive.

Inadequate Words

These chaotic times
Words are inadequate

Images swirl and collide in my mind
mirroring the chaos of the day

Oceans rage
Seas roar
Clouds charge through the heavens
Sweltering heat pierces the earth and penetrates man
Swirling winds stir the heavens and oceans
Until heaving themselves against the inhabitants of the
shorelines
Disrupting once tranquil lives

Lightning strikes as a spear
Thrown from the heavens to the earth
The target is hit
Contact and explosion commingle
Flames ignite
And so a fire is born
Racing across the earth
Scorching all in its path

Man screams at man
Individual perspective reigns supreme
Each shuts his ears and brain
The mind shrinks as does the sphere of influence

Days trudge through time
Moving from one to the next
When will this slumber end
So the foliage of spring and new life can break forth
Then one speculates why life seems so shallow

Renaissance Fair

Cassie pushed through the crowd, rounding the corner. Her breathing was heavy and heart pounding. She clutched a satchel and kept turning her head to scan the crowd behind her. People around her were laughing and joking as they meandered down the street. *Darn, why won't these folks just get moving,* she thought.

"Excuse me, excuse me," Cassie kept saying as she edged her way between people.

"What's your rush, lady?"

"Don't be so rude."

"You're too pushy."

She heard people curse at her while she continued pushing through the crowd.

I have to leave here. If Ted discovers I've taken the satchel, he'll kill me.

Cassie rounded the corner and thought she saw a glimpse of Ted. She ducked into the first storefront she saw. Panting, she tried to calm her thoughts, while she slowed her walking to not draw attention to herself. She moved casually through the various departments until she came to the lingerie area. She went to the fitting room after selecting some items because Ted wouldn't enter the lingerie department. There, she'd be able to think. She sank into the chair after closing the door.

Her head was in her hands and she sobbed.

"What will I do with this cash?"

While Cassie sat in the fitting room, she remembered Stephen, a friend who worked for the government. She pondered how she might be able to contact him and remembered the local renaissance fair being hosted by the city. It was a week-long event, and Stephen always worked the event.

He joked with her many times, saying, "You never know what type of characters will show up at these festivals."

Cassie pulled out her phone to research what she could wear as a disguise.

She scanned the store and saw no sign of Ted, so she moved to the cosmetic area where she selected dark eye shadow and make-up darker than her skin tone. From there she went to the costume jewelry area, where she found some thin silver bangles, several leather bands and a couple of beaded bracelets. After securing her purchases, she left the store via the alley to find the local costume shop.

The costume shop was filled with renaissance clothing. Much of it was either beautiful and elegant, or more simplistic. Cassie wanted something out of character. She wanted a skirt, not a short one, but one which would cover her knees. She loved the look of the high boots, but knew she needed flat boots. When she found a pair of boots that were in her size and comfortable, she was thrilled. The entire time she was selecting her costume, she evaluated if she'd be able to run in the outfit or if the clothing provided anything, another could use to grab her.

She settled on a handkerchief style skirt with a patchwork pattern combining a shimmery green material, a red print and white broadcloth. The skirt had two triangular aprons tied around the waist. The pantaloons she found to wear under the skirt worked well with the boots. She located a white off the shoulders crop top and a complimentary green corset top. She found a sturdy belt and a large pouch she could attach to it. The pouch was actually for a pirate costume, but Cassie needed something large. The shop had some dark curly hair extension. She selected those with a dark turquoise colored head wrap which tied in the back.

While in the fitting room, she applied the make-up, moved the rolls of cash from the satchel into the pouch, placed a hankie over the cash and dropped her wallet, identification and cell phone on top. She took her clothes and jewelry and stuffed them into the satchel. Cassie figured she would stop at the nearby train station and rent a storage locker before heading to the festival grounds.

The clerk whistled, long and slow, when she stepped out of the fitting room.

"Wow, lady. You look different from the person who walked into the shop. You look like a gypsy or a fortune teller. Allow me to gift you a small crystal ball to match your get-up."

"Thanks. I hadn't thought of that, but it's exactly what I need."

She flashed a big smile and paid the clerk. After securing a storage locker, she used a private restroom, where she sent Stephen a cryptic message. She hoped he would decipher it. They'd been friends a long time; he always said if she needed help, to think of him. He would be there for her.

The return message from Stephen came before she reached the festival's entrance gate. It said, "I'm the pirate with the red headscarf and black eye patch. Meet me mid street by the fortune teller's booth."

Cassie sighed. Soon she wouldn't feel so all alone.

She paid her entrance fee and entered the gate. Between those in costume and those who happened upon the fair, it was crowded and noisy. Wafts of grilled meat hung in the air, and occasionally she caught a scent of sweet confections. Cassie found it all somewhat overwhelming. At first, she smiled at seeing the different costumes. She watched jugglers working the crowd and walking close to people. Vendors approached those in civilian dress, attempting to sell their wares. She even saw a couple in royal costume stoop down to talk with children. It was then she realized they could be anyone, even Ted. With this reminder, she hustled toward the main path and saw Stephen standing like some swash buckling pirate.

"Hey matey," she called.

He turned and smiled.

"Are you here to replace the fortune teller on site? May I have my fortune told tonight?"

Cassie laughed.

"It is rather funny you selected this location. No, I'm not a replacement fortune teller, but yes. I'd be happy to tell your fortune. Is there somewhere a little more private than the thorough fare so I don't disclose your secrets?"

Stephen stepped back to look at Cassie. "I didn't recognize you at first. There's a bench under the trees off the walkway. There may be several booths in the area, but sufficiently removed from the bench so we won't be heard. Shall we head there?"

Cassie glanced around again and nodded in agreement.

"Girl, you have to relax a little. A gypsy should be in control or slightly wild. You look like you're expecting a ghost or something."

They settled on the bench and Cassie moved in close. She took Stephen's hand and turned it over in hers, revealing his palm.

"Wow. You're really going to do a palm reading session? Can't wait to hear what you've got to say."

Speaking quietly, but with authority, Cassie continued.

"Stephen, today is an incredibly important day. You are going to happen upon a lot of money, considerably more than you expected. However, with this money comes risk and danger. Both to you and anyone else who knows about the money. Are you up for the challenge?"

Stephen pulled back his hand and laughed. He gazed at his palm; studied Cassie and, for the first time, recognized how serious she looked. There was no smile. No hint this was a game. She looked him directly in the eyes.

"This is a joke, right? You're not serious, are you? You're just playing the role, right?"

Slowly, Cassie shook her head no.

"What the heck? What are you trying to tell me? Do you know something?"

She took his hand again and revealed his palm. Using her index finger of her other hand, she traced one crevice while she spoke.

"This is not a joke. We need to make this look real, in the event anyone is watching us. I'm in trouble. Are you up for the challenge?"

Stephen shook his head yes.

"Tell me what I need to do. Are you safe?" he said.

Cassie scanned the park area and path without moving.

"For the moment. We need to go somewhere private; make it look like it is part of the festival activities."

"Right on. I can do that."

Stephen stood to his feet and pulled Cassie up beside him.

"Ma'am, that was the best fortune reading I've ever had. I want to celebrate with you."

He put his arm around Cassie and pulled her close. Still holding her close, he jigged down the street.

"Come-on lady. Loosen up. We're gonna party."

Under his breath, he told her they were going to dance toward the gate and leave. And he wanted it to appear like they had been enjoying a swell time.

Cassie joined in the merriment and the two danced down the path. They waved goodbye to the ticket sellers as they passed through the gate. Still skipping down the sidewalk, they approached a car.

Stephen said, "This is my car. Hop in, my lady, and we'll figure out what comes next."

Cassie curtsied and slid into the car seat. After Stephen closed the car door she immediately locked it, then settled her skirt, waiting for Stephen to get in behind the wheel. Cassie kept scanning the street, looking for Ted.

Stephen pulled the door shut and took a long look in Cassie's direction.

"Girl. I don't know what is happening, but you must relax or you're going to draw attention to us. Take a deep breath. Let's get away from downtown and find somewhere quiet to talk."

Cassie sucked in a deep breath and let it out slowly.

"You ok now?"

As they pulled away from the sidewalk and got further away from the city streets, Cassie started to relax in her seat.

"I don't know exactly where to start. Today has been like no other."

"How about you start at the beginning? Or at least start at the beginning of what caused you to contact me."

Cassie replayed the events of the day. She was the only employee still in the front office when the dark featured foreign guy showed up. He barely looked at her. It seemed a little strange to see him carrying the same satchel as hers, but didn't give it anymore consideration. He dropped his satchel on the floor next to hers and went into Ted's office, where he closed the glass door. She was running late, and wanted to see a movie tonight, so in her rush, she must have grabbed the wrong satchel. The man yelled at Ted to shoot her before she gets away, and Ted jumped up from his desk. She ran out the door and darted down the street. She explained how she eluded him by slipping into the department store. It was in the fitting room where she discovered the satchel was full of hundred-dollar bills rolled into bundles. The discovery led to contacting Stephen.

"I don't know what to do. I heard his visitor say to kill me, and I was frightened, so I ran. Then I saw Ted frantically searching for me in the crowd. I'm terrified."

"Where's the satchel? How much money was in the bag? What did you do with the money?"

"My stuff and the satchel are in a locker at the train station. I have the money with me. I didn't count the money. It's all bundles of hundred-dollar bills rolled."

"Ohhhh."

"Can you describe Ted well enough for someone to draw a sketch?"

"I… I think so."

"Good. I think I should take you to headquarters. We need to talk with the detectives on duty about your safety. I'll have someone else go to the train station to retrieve your belongings. I think it's best we keep you under wraps until we have a more thorough understanding of who we are searching for and what is happening here."

Stephen kept driving. He turned down an alley and then into an underground parking facility.

"I don't recall ever being in this part of town," said Cassie.

"I bet not. This is a secure entrance into the station house. No one can enter the garage without a special transponder."

Stephen walked around and helped Cassie out of the car. Once again she breathed anxiously with her eyes darting around, wondering *what have I gotten myself into?*

Travel Writing

Body weary
Heart full
Brain whirring

Goodbyes said
Home calling
Days between

Wheels turning
Farmland images blur
Topography changes
Jagged rocks erupt
Uninhabited rugged skyline
Layer upon layer
Clouds race across the heavens
Like us
Racing down highways

The ascent begins
The Rockies tower before us
Geography requires
Slower pace

Scars of earlier fires
Proudly display their destruction
Boasting the power they exert upon the land

Once sleepy mountain towns
Sprang back to life
As hordes of people moved west
And tourists clamored
To see the sights

Urban centers know no borders
As house upon house is built
People and vehicles abound

Descents and ascents
Come in rapid succession
Topography changes once more
Gone is the lush green
Of Midwestern farmland
Replaced by ruggedness
Boulders rise from the ground
Varied vegetation proudly
Displays its fight for life
In this arid land

In our absence we missed
The scorching heat
And the long-awaited rain
Our house shouts
Welcome home!

The Requests

Their father had two requests before he died.

They had met with him yesterday. They talked, listened as he spoke, and rode back to their respective homes together, fully expecting to have another opportunity to question his requests.

The unexpected call from the hospital, informing them their father had died in the night, upended those plans. They each drove to the hospital. Mere minutes separated their arrival. The doctor ushered them into the conference room, explained the circumstances of their father's passing and suggested they may each want a few minutes alone with him. Dr. Connors said he would do his rounds and be available in a couple of hours for further questions.

The two entered his hospital room. The sterile room was where their father spent his final two weeks. He didn't want to be here. In fact, he hated it here. He despised people telling him what he could and could not do; hated others dictating what he would eat and when; and that they kept running endless tests on him, but couldn't explain what was wrong with him.

He entered the emergency room because he didn't feel well. He was weak, could barely stand, and almost could not speak. The neighbor had brought him, insisting he needed care. He was unprepared to learn his blood sugars were grossly elevated, and they admitted him to stabilize his sugars and for observation. Allison was the first to receive word her dad was in the hospital. She contacted Karen, and the two went to the hospital together. Dad was a cantankerous man. He was strong willed and didn't stand for anyone telling him what to do. Allison and Karen had long since learned to live independent lives visiting their father for holidays and other special days throughout the year. Karen saw him less frequently than Allison. She found it easier to keep him at a distance. He was critical whenever he came to her house. Karen left his presence feeling like she didn't measure up and never found out what he expected.

Then yesterday, he told them what he wanted after he died. He made them promise to ensure all his paperwork and his guns were out of the house before anyone else was allowed on the premises. Okay, they both thought they could handle this request. It was the second request which left them baffled. He wanted his sports car to be washed and detailed, then he wanted to be buried in his car. He assured the girls he finalized all the financial arrangements. They only had to find the paperwork.

They both found the request vain, extravagant, and just like their father. But they figured they could talk him out of this during their next visit. Only they never had the opportunity. He died first.

They each said their private goodbyes to the man who had been their father. After planning for the Funeral Home to pick up the body, the girls drove to their family home. They were on a mission. They had to find the paperwork relative to their father's burial arrangements. Allison looked at Karen.

"How hard can this be? We know Dad has a filing cabinet. We'll peruse the files to find what we need. I still can't believe his sweet little car will be in the ground. What a selfish man."

"Yeah," said Karen.

After entering the house, Karen went directly to the filing cabinet.

"Oh, no. This is going to be difficult."

Allison said, "What do you mean?"

"Come here and look at this."

Both girls stared in amazement as they looked at the full filing cabinet drawer. There were no file folders. Just envelopes, each dated and placed in the drawer by date sequence. All the drawers were the same.

"Where do we start?" said Allison.

"I don't know. But let's find something to drink before we start this process."

"Great idea. I'll get us something."

Allison disappeared into the kitchen. Karen could hear her opening cupboards.

"Found it," said Allison.

Karen rushed into the kitchen.

"Really? I expected it would take a little longer than this," said Karen.

"No silly. I found glasses. The task is larger than we expected. Look in the cupboard over there."

Karen looked and her heart sunk. Their father had taken to filing paperwork in the cupboards and the filing cabinet. Based on the dates on the envelopes. the newer mail was in the cupboard.

"Yikes! Let's have that drink and get started."

They popped the wine cork and pulled a stack of papers out of the cupboard, and sat at the kitchen table. It didn't take long to recognize their father had kept every piece of mail he received, dating each and then placing it in a cupboard or the filing cabinet. There appeared to be nothing too insignificant. He kept everything. They found political pieces, personal letters, solicitations from various businesses, and financial communication. Karen suggested they make a quick pass through the documents and dispose of the obvious junk, like political pieces, and advertisements. They agreed to keep anything related to financial institutions, legal papers, bills and things connected to work or medical issues. The girls worked through stacks of paper, creating piles for the various topics and tossing the political and advertisement pieces.

They found the project tedious. Yet, the girls were amused their father kept some of the things he had. Some were merely advertising fliers. It took several days and multiple bottles of wine to complete the initial pass through of the paperwork. They found the documentation and were shocked by the extensive arrangements their father had made for his burial. Upon seeing the details, the girls decided to honor his burial plans, but only have a small memorial service with no viewing of the body. The mortician had already explained the process involved for placing him in the driver's seat of his old t-bird. It was difficult for the girls to maintain propriety when talking about these arrangements. They each had images from an old movie, *Weekend at Bernie's* and feared if they gazed at one another while at the Funeral Home, they would burst out laughing. The mortician, Mr. Banks, would give them a stern look and shake his head, all while muttering something about their father warning him of the two girls.

Allison and Karen spent more time together and realized they enjoyed being together. They were grateful for the healing found during this process. After finalizing the arrangements for the memorial service, the girls had agreed not to share the details of the burial, as they found their father's request ostentatious. Any explanation they could muster up felt inadequate for such an action.

Other than the mess regarding the paperwork, everything in their father's house was neat and orderly. Yet they had not located the guns. In fact, they couldn't agree if he had guns. Allison had never seen them. Karen vaguely remembered him speaking of them at dinner once. So, the girls continued searching through the house. When they started removing his clothes from the closet, they saw a cupboard on the back wall. Upon opening in, they found four pairs of antique dueling pistols.

Karen said, "What the heck did he have these for?"

Allison said, "Good question. What will we do with them?"

"Yeah. Good question."

The girls met with an attorney to start all the processes required by the state after one dies. They were tasked with identifying and appraising everything on the property. Even the attorney was stymied regarding the t-bird. It would no longer exist after they buried it with their father. It was decided not to list it on the property inventory.

The church graciously hosted the memorial service and a luncheon afterwards. Cousins and relatives the girls hadn't seen in years attended the event. It was a pleasant memorial service, and during lunch, many attendees shared fun stories about their father. The day preceded well until Chester approached Allison.

"Say Allison. We haven't seen one another in years. Sorry about your dad. But what is happening with his t-bird? It was a beauty, and I'd give my eye-teeth for an opportunity to own his car."

Allison sputtered and stammered, but no words came out. Suddenly she started crying, said she was sorry and ran to the ladies restroom.

The room grew still. Chester was the center of attention. He looked from one face to another. He shrugged and said, "I don't know what happened. I just asked about Uncle's car."

An older man walked up to Chester. "You know, sonny, that car was Ted's pride and joy. I don't think we should talk about it today."

"But, but…"

"No buts. We're not here to discuss Ted's car. Leave it alone and don't go upsetting the girls," said Herb.

No one seemed to notice how long Allison remained in the bathroom. The oldest people paid their respects and left first. Others gathered in groups, talking and laughing before they said their goodbyes. Karen saw Chester approaching her. She glanced around to determine if anyone was near. Finding no one close by, she put on a smile and stood still. Chester approached her.

"I'm sorry to have upset Allison."

Karen said, "It's been an exhausting week. Allison will eventually be fine."

"Say, can we talk about the car?"

"Actually, no. We've had a lot to deal with and today was more emotional than I expected. I don't want to discuss Dad's stuff."

"Okay. Okay, I get it. I just want it on record that I want first dibs on his car."

Karen shrugged and said, "Noted."

Chester looked at her, grinned, and said his goodbyes.

After everyone left, the girls were left standing in the fellowship hall of the church alone surveying the mementoes. There were several ladies in the kitchen cleaning up from the lunch. One of them called out to the girls.

"Are you okay? There's plenty of food left, why don't you take some home?"

`The girls thanked these women for their help and each left with several plates of food and desserts. The next few weeks were a succession of days, each looking very similar to the last. Work during the day at their respective jobs, getting takeout, and meeting at dad's house to continue going through things. Weekends involved moving things to thrift stores or the men's shelter. They reduced his stuff to his tools, furniture, and household objects. The girls picked out items they wanted and took them home including two pairs of pistols each. Previously, they had scheduled a meeting with a gun dealer specializing in antiquities. This meeting left the girls flabbergasted at the value of the guns; they decided it was wise to remove the weapons from an empty house. The purchase receipts they found proved the guns were a good investment for their father. They contacted an estate sales company to learn how to liquidate the rest of the items within the house.

The day of the burial arrived, and both girls met Mr. Banks at the burial site. There was a backhoe standing beside the gaping hole. The transport pulled up and carefully offloaded the t-bird. Mr. Banks had arranged for their father to be in the driver's seat with his hands on the steering wheel. It was quite a sight, and neither girl knew how to react. Should they laugh; should they cry? Allison and Karen avoided making eye contact. The transport driver carefully lowered the car into the hole. Each girl dropped a bouquet on the car after Mr. Banks recited a few words. The backhoe began filling in the hole. Mr. Banks turned to the girls.

"I'm sorry for your loss. Your father was an interesting man, and this certainly was the most unusual funeral request I've ever fulfilled. The headstone you selected should be available within the next sixty days. I'll contact you when we get it placed. I wish you both well. Good day."

"Thank you and goodbye."

Mr. Banks was gone before either could say anymore. The girls stood and watched the ending processes of leveling the ground and the backhoe being loaded onto the transport which had minutes before carried the t-bird to this site. They finally looked at each other. Allison had tears running down her cheeks, yet she was laughing. Karen joined in the laughter. The girls hugged.

"I don't know how I'm supposed to feel. Today did not feel real," said Allison.

"I'm struggling with the same thoughts. No one is buried in a car. I mean, he did look like himself sitting behind the wheel. It was in that car where he was the happiest," said Karen.

"I know. But what's our response when quizzed about the car? You know, Chester can be persistent."

Karen was silent for a minute.

Allison said, "Did you hear me? What's our response when others inquire about the car?"

"I heard you. I'm thinking. It has to be believable and end the inquiries."

"Yeah. I don't want it to haunt us."

"Let's find a restaurant for lunch. We can talk about this there."

"Sounds like a good plan," said Karen.

After a last glance at the site, the girls walked down the road. They discussed telling people they didn't know what their dad did with the car; he got rid of the car before he went into the hospital. Or they could reveal the truth and not answer questions. They couldn't decide what to say after talking about the pros and cons.

While sorting Dad's personal items, the girls spent several evenings at the house. They often picked up carry-out for dinner and brought a bottle or two of wine with them. During those evenings, they relived their childhood and shared their memories. Allison found it fascinating how they each remembered different things. They grew up in the same house, but their recollections were different. Their mom had died young after a skittish horse threw her while riding. Their dad never rode again. He wasn't the same after her accident. His car became his passion, and he pulled further and further away from the girls until they rarely saw him. Sorting their dad's property and getting the house ready to sell required the girls to spend more time at the house. More time than they had spent there after leaving home as adults.

After removing all personal items from the house, Dad's property was listed for sale. Allison resumed her normal schedule at work. Karen gave notice at her job so she could figure out what she wanted to do. What she hadn't done was disclose to Allison how much money she made selling her half of the guns. It was quite a windfall, and they had not yet sold the house.

She hadn't decided if she would return to work or not. The girls hadn't spoken of the car since they lowered it into the ground.

The house sold; their attorney completed all the paperwork and scheduled a meeting for the girls to sign the final documents. It was a somber meeting. The girls reviewed the paperwork. Allison sat there in shock, looking at the final numbers.

Karen said, "Are you alright? You know, dad always claimed there was enough to care for us."

Allison gulped.

"Yeah. I just never knew."

They signed the papers and went to the local bistro for dinner and a drink.

Allison arrived home later in the evening to discover Chester left a message wanting to know the disposition of the car and expressing his interest again. He said he would call later.

Oh, great! Not him again. Allison stewed as she paced around her house. She was still trying to grasp the truth her father was dead, and had left her a sizable estate. She did not know her father had amassed such a fortune. Other than his t-bird, he lived like a miser. He was grumpy and always accusing others of trying to obtain his money. She knew she didn't want to be like her dad. When the phone rang, she was still pondering the day's events. She answered without glancing to see who was calling.

"Hi Allison. Chester here. I hope you listened to my last message."

Allison swallowed hard.

"Yes. I did. I just walked in the door."

"My, but you're out late on a work night," said Chester.

Allison could feel the irritation rise within her. *Who did he think he was to question how she lived her life?* She paused and smiled before she spoke.

"It was a lovely evening, Chester. What can I do for you?"

"You can tell me how much you want for you dad's car. I'll take it off your hands. It'll get the same care from me as from your dad. Just name your price and I'll pay!"

Without thinking, the words just spilled out.

"Well Chester, you're too late. Dad has the car with him."

"Wha… What? What do you mean, the car is with Ted?"

"Literally, the car was buried with dad."

Chester burst into laughter, then after a pause, became somber.

"Come on Allison. Let's get serious here. I don't want to play games. I just want the car. Your old man loved that vehicle and babied it. It was his prized possession. All the car folks are talking about who's going to be driving it. I want to be that person!"

"I am serious. The joke is on you, Chester. We buried dad in the car. I don't want to talk about it anymore."

Allison disconnected the call and then rang her sister.

"Hi. Didn't you get enough of me today?"

Karen laughed.

Allison said, "Yeah. It was a remarkable day until I arrived home and received a call from Chester. I can't believe how arrogant he can be. I guess he pushed my buttons, and I spilled the beans about dad being buried in the car."

"Oh."

There was a lengthy pause as the truth of the message sank in.

Karen said, "I guess we'll just have to deal with the fall out. I was thinking we could protect dad's memory, but didn't know how to do so without creating a big lie. And I know we both struggle with telling lies. It was his wish, and he got it. So, we shouldn't feel any guilt or remorse about his choices."

"Yeah, you're right. I'm sorry we didn't talk before I spouted off."

"It's okay. It's no secret amongst the family how Chester is. We probably won't hear from him again for a long time. Are you going to be okay tonight?"

"Yeah. I'm tired. I think I'll just call it a night. We can talk later."

"Okay. Goodnight, Love you."

"Love you too. Goodnight."

Island Lessons

Growing up in the heartland
surrounded by rolling farmlands
Books filled my days
Adventure on the horizon

Islands brought dreams of
Mystic
Adventure
Romance
Withdrawal from day to day life

Dreams replaced with responsibilities
Promise of islands
occasionally surfaced
in thoughts of escape

Always still holding the promise of
Adventure
Mystic
Romance

Explored a few
Washington Island
Kent Island
Barrier Islands off Charleston
Alcatraz Island
Coronado
Mackinac

Ireland
England

Beautiful
yes
Romantic
some
Historic
many
Adventurous
some
Culture
all different

Enchant my heart
Not so much

Lessons learned
Beauty abounds everywhere
Culture captivates my heart
History fascinates
And forms culture
Culture affects individuals
People captivate my heart
Relationships matter

A Day in 2050

The wind is blowing, the blue-sky fades to grey close to the horizon.

From a distance out in the water appears a line of dark triangular features. As the girls moved closer, these triangles transformed to form a line of men perched on their surfboards, all awaiting the perfect wave.

Wendy Wilson and her friend Sara Gentry wanted to relax for the afternoon, so they headed to the beach. All appeared harmless as they watched the various surfers catch a wave, ride it, then tumble into the water. Some were athletic, others were more acrobatic in their movements. The combination of the men's maneuvers, the ocean breeze, warming sun, and the roar of the ocean as waves crashed was mesmerizing. The girls, also known as WW and SG, chatted, marveling at how long it had been since they'd seen men surfing. Older family members spoke of days they would race to the beach after work, or for the weekend to enjoy endless days in the sun and water. Wendy and Sara struggled to imagine such a life.

They noticed how few people were on the beach, but failed to notice the large black van like structures parked closest to the water. Few people were at the pier today. The girls continued to speak of the old family tales they heard as children; of how this was a tourist attraction; individuals from around the earth traveled here to enjoy the weather and ocean. There were fishermen on the pier today; but no tourists.

They relaxed, knowing it would be awhile before they could enjoy this again. As the sun prepared to dip below the horizon, the tide was pummeling the beach and temperatures were dropping.

WW looked at SG before she spoke.

"I think we should return to the house. You know, we must be there before dark."

"Yeah, I suppose."

The girls walked back to their vehicle, a dark grey hover craft. WW touched the roof of the vehicle and the sides lifted like wings, allowing the girls to strap themselves into their seats. Before they could say anything, the vehicle lifted from the ground and glided through the air. As they approached the house, doors to the parking structure lifted. As soon as the hover craft slid under the doors. These same doors automatically closed. The girls exited the vehicle and entered the house.

SG always marveled at how WW was allowed to live in her grandparents' house. Most of her friends lived in small apartments stacked one on top of each another, with no opportunity for other housing arrangements. The word on the street was WW's grandmother was some important person in the technology field, having developed a wonder product for the government. So, the government allowed the family to retain the house. And thus, now WW had her grandmother's house. WW also did technology work for the government, but on a limited basis. She spent most of her time in the garden surrounding the house. Fruit producing trees were everywhere. There was a vegetable garden and herbs grew on the back deck. Sure, the drones would deliver a daily supply of eggs, dairy and protein; the property provided for most of WW's other needs.

They had barely begun preparations for dinner when the alarm went off in the house and a message started blaring over the system.

"Attention! Attention! We have been invaded. Please remain within your premises. Residents are on lock down until we apprehend the invaders."

Aircraft were flying overhead and spotlights were scanning the area.

"Oh no. This means I'm not going home tonight," said SG.

"No worries. The guest room is always ready and I've got plenty of food. We can get fresh fruit in the yard. We'll be okay. You should get comfortable, there are clothes upstairs."

"How long will this last?"

"No idea. It has been years since this happened."

SG went upstairs to see what she could find for clothes while WW began prepping food for dinner. The screen on the dining room wall popped to life and broadcasted the day's events. WW gasped and dropped the kitchen knife when she saw an image of her and SG walking back to the hover craft. She stood there, gazing at the screen. Immediately after the girls walked past the camera, she could see surfers coming out of the water. The men were seen loading their equipment before getting into the black vehicles. WW sat in front of the screen when the following announcement was made. Supposedly, the men had rendezvoused with others already on the land. They surrounded the city and locked off all entrance and exits points.

"SG, come here. Are you watching the announcement?"

When SG entered the dining area, it was obvious she had changed into clothing more comfortable, which she discovered in the closet in the guest room.

"What's going on? I haven't been watching the news?"

WW retold what she learned from the report.

"They captured us on camera leaving the beach. We almost didn't make it out of town."

"Great. What does that mean for us?"

WW said, "Undoubtedly, they'll come checking to make sure I'm home. There will be questions and an interrogation. I'm almost sure of this."

While fixing dinner, the girls heard the hover craft and other flying vehicles overhead. Suddenly, a voice rang out through the sound system.

"Wendy Wilson and whoever is with you, you need to come out front with your hands on your head. Stand in front of the house and remain there until you have been cleared."

"What the heck," said SG.

"Come-on. Let's just do as we've been told."

The girls exited through the front door and stood on the path in front of the house with their hands on their heads. A small drone like hover craft flew around them, pausing in front of each of them and shining a light into their eyes. While this happened, a larger hover craft flew over the house several times, before flying away. A mechanical like voice emitted from the small drone telling the girls it had cleared them and they could re-enter the home. They were reminded they could not leave, nor could they allow anyone to enter.

SG said, "What…"

She looked at WW and froze. Never had WW appeared so stern and angry. She didn't dare to speak another word.

The voice from the hover craft continued.

"Heat seeking review of the house completed. No additional living bodies within. Return to the house and remain until the all clear is issued."

They lowered their hands. SG stared at WW, who shrugged and said, "Let's get back inside and finish dinner."

SG wondered what had just happened, and what did WW know about all of this?

Habits

Habits creep in like stalkers at night
We awake and find them amongst us

So goes the way of the news
Read for interest or to be informed
Look for more complete details
Shock value captivates attention

Research
Then repeat
And repeat
Peace disrupted
Habit revealed

I long to return to consuming news
On a "need to know" basis

Yet still struggle with the question
How to be informed yet not addicted

The Living Doll

Marian was preparing dinner when Sabine came running into the kitchen.

"Mama, there is a beautiful doll on my bed. She's talking to me. Where did she come from?"

"Sabine, slow down. She is a beautiful doll. What are you going to name her?"

"She told me her name is Samantha."

Marian struggled to hide her amusement.

"Honey, Samantha is a lovely name. Are you sure that's what you want to call her?"

"Mama. She told me her name is Samantha. How did she get here?"

Sabine stomped her foot and became serious.

"Mama. I don't understand how she got here."

Marian had observed Sabine becoming overly dramatic and withdrawn the last few weeks and hoped a beautiful doll might calm her down and help her focus. She sighed. Resigned, she realized this was no better than the other toys she had tried. She turned to Sabine.

"Honey, I saw the beautiful doll in an antique store window when in town shopping today. I remembered how much you loved dolls when you were younger, and how interested you were in history, so I thought you would find her interesting."

"Oh, Mama, she is interesting. Do you know any more about her?"

Sabine was calm and focused. Marian was comfortable telling her what she discovered from the shopkeeper.

"The shopkeeper told me she was wrapped in tissue paper in an old trunk. The trunk was in the attic of an grand old home in upstate New York. The owners had been from a wealthy family. When they died, there were no living relatives. Therefore, everything went up for auction. The shopkeeper bid on the trunk and took it back to his shop. People are searching for trunks."

"Mama, I don't care about the trunk. I want to know about Samantha."

"Okay, okay. The doll…."

"It's Samantha."

"Okay, Samantha was found in the trunk when the shopkeeper opened the trunk in his store. He didn't deal in toys, so he fluffed up her dress and put her in the window this very morning. I walked by and was captivated by how exquisite she looked. So I purchased her."

"Okay."

"Her clothing style suggests early colonial life, but the porcelain face and painted details look like something from early French doll makers."

"Oh. I knew she was old. Mama, we have to figure out how she got into the trunk."

"Well Sabine, I'm making dinner. Your father will be home soon. Why don't you combine the doll with your curiosity and write a story explaining where she came from?"

"Okay," said Sabine, as she turned and ran back upstairs.

For the first time, Marian smiled. It had been over a year since Sabine was interested in anything. Maybe life would return to normal. She was pleased she purchased the doll and gave little thought to the details of their conversation as she completed preparations for dinner. When Bill came home, Marian pulled him into the kitchen to tell him about the change in Sabine's behavior.

"Honey, thanks for sharing this good news. I can't wait to hear what Sabine has to tell us at dinner."

Marian called everyone when dinner was ready. Bill arrived from the den where he was working, and Sabine came bounding down the stairs. Her parents noticed her cheeks were flushed when she plopped into her chair.

Marian said, "Are you feeling okay?"

"Sure, why?" said Sabine.

"No reason, just checking."

Bill and Marian exchanged glances, and Sabine just stared at them.

Bill cleared his throat. Then said, "Your mom says you have a new doll. What did you name her?"

Sabine stared at her mom.

"Didn't you tell him? Her name is Samantha. Why do you keep thinking I named her? She told me Samantha is her name."

"Oh, okay. I must have misunderstood or not been listening clearly when your mom was talking about today. What can you tell me about... You said Samantha is her name?"

Sabine perked up and smiled at her father.

"Yeah, Dad. Her name is Samantha. She said the last thing she remembered was her friend Brenda hugged her, kissed her and set her on her bed before leaving for the day."

"Ah, ha," said Dad.

"Well, Brenda never came back. Her mom walked into the room, looked around, and cried. She would close the door and leave Samantha in there all alone. Uniformed men searched the room one day. One of them even picked up Samantha, turned her in lots of different directions and peaked under her dress before dropping her back on the bed. Doors were slammed and Samantha heard lots of crying. Samantha was scared."

"It sounds scary."

Bill glanced at Marian, who was busy clearing the table and only appeared to be partially listening to this tale.

"Sabine continued by saying, one day the mother came in the room and started packing up Brenda's clothes. Just before closing the trunk, she picked up Samantha and hugged the doll and snuggled her. Then she dropped her into the trunk on top of Brenda's clothing, shut the lid and the latched clicked shut. It was dark and Samantha could not hear much, but as she jostled amongst the clothing, she felt afraid. She heard a faint clomping noise and then a loud thump as she bounced around in the trunk. Things became quiet and dark. She had no sense of time."

Bill asked, "Does Samantha know when this happened?"

"No. She hasn't. She didn't know of any events until the shop keeper opened the trunk and lifted her out. He whistled and said that she was a beauty. But he didn't know her name. He placed her on a bench in his window. She watched people come by and stare at her. Then mom went in the store and bought her."

"That she did."

"Samantha is excited to be part of the family. Oh Dad, I'm so glad she is mine."

Marian smiled at Sabine.

"We're glad she's part of your life, as well. I'm happy to see you excited about something again. Don't you think you should get ready for bed?"

"Sure."

Sabine bounded up the stairs. Marian looked at Bill.

She said, "What do you think?"

"I don't know what to think. I'm glad to see my little girl back. It has been difficult looking at her and seeing her so disinterested in life and shutting everyone out. But really, Marian, a talking doll? Where does she get her ideas?"

"I don't know. We should talk with her doctor about this, but I'd like to savor a few days enjoying having our daughter back. I think I can go along with this ruse of a talking doll. What about you?"

Bill said, "I'm with you. Let's see what a couple of days brings. Maybe she'll lose interest in the doll. What did she say the name was again?"

"Samantha."

"Yeah, Samantha. Perhaps she'll lose interest in Samantha and pick up interest in something else, like one of her old friends."

"Maybe. It would be nice."

Bill said, "Let's keep an open mind for a couple of days. Then decide if we want to talk to her doctor."

After turning off the lights, they went upstairs. They peeked into Sabine's room and saw she was asleep with Samantha snuggled next to her. They went to their room, smiling.

The next morning, after Bill and Sabine left, Marian put away the laundry. When she entered the Sabine's room, she was humming. She stopped and looked around the room. It surprised her to see Sabine had picked up all her toys. Her dirty laundry was in the hamper and her bed was made with Samantha propped against the bed pillows. She smiled before saying to herself.

"This is such a pleasant change."

Then she heard something. A faint voice appeared to be talking.

"What is so pleasant?"

Marian turned to look out the door. Then she spun around in the bedroom. Where was this voice coming from? She wondered, am I losing my mind? I thought I heard something. After setting the laundry on the bed, Marian left the room, shaking her head.

At the end of the school day, Sabine burst through the front door and ran straight upstairs to her bedroom. Marian heard her door slam shut and wondered what had happened at school. There were cookies in the oven, so she remained in the kitchen tending to her baking. Before the cookies were off the baking sheet, Sabine stomped into the kitchen and glared at her mom.

"Why didn't you put my laundry away?"

"What are you talking about?" said Marian.

"My room was clean this morning. Why didn't you put my clothes away for me?"

"Ah, yes. Your room was cleaned. It looked spectacular. Thank you. I got distracted when I brought the clothes in. I guess I forgot to return and take care of the task. You always wanted to put your clothes away, so I didn't think twice."

"Oh. You're right. I guess I have asked you to let me put my own things away. I was startled because things didn't look how I'd left them. Sorry. Say, mind if I try one of your cookies? They smell great."

"Sure. What do you think about us each getting a drink and enjoying a snack together?"

"Sure!"

Sabine ran to the cupboard and retrieved glasses and plates for both of them. Marian pulled the milk container from the refrigerator and filled the glasses, while Sabine placed two cookies on each of the plates. Then she carried them to the table.

Marian smiled as she remembered the last time they had enjoyed a treat together. It seemed like ages ago. Ever since the violent outbreak at school, Sabine had withdrawn and wouldn't talk with anyone. Her answers were short staccato replies, providing no opportunity for further discussion. Even the doctor had failed to pull her out of her shell. This was a good day.

They talked about the day at school while enjoying cookies. Marian said she needed to continue preparing dinner.

Sabine said, "Great. I'm going back upstairs. See you at dinner."

When Bill returned home, Marian shared with him the afternoon events. She had already forgotten about hearing the voice in Sabine's bedroom, so she said nothing about that. They both reveled in the fact their daughter might be returning to her normal self. Marian set the table for the evening meal and Bill called Sabine to the table. Conversation was pleasant during the meal with Sabine, even sharing with her father how she helped another student with one of their tough math problems. Bill and Sabine were talking about math when Marian went upstairs. She saw the light on in Sabine's room. That's odd. She usually turns her lights off when she leaves, thought Marian. Marian entered Sabine's room and was again struck by how clean and organized everything. She could see Sabine's schoolbooks laid out on the desk. Smiling, she turned to leave the room.

She heard the small, faint voice again. Only this time, it seemed more demanding.

"Why do you act so surprised when you enter this room?"

Marian stared into the room. She strode to the bed and stared at the doll.

"Were you talking to me?"

She felt foolish talking out loud to a doll. And was astonished by the reply.

"Of course I'm talking to you. Is anyone else in this room?"

Marian hurried out of the room. She rushed down the stairs and burst into the dining room.

"Mama, are you alright?" said Sabine.

Marian slumped into her chair. Her face was ashen. She looked at Bill.

Then said, "Will you fix me a cup of coffee?"

"Sure, are you alright?"

Marian shrugged. Bill returned to the dining room with a cup of coffee.

"Are you ready to tell us what's going on?" said Bill.

"Yeah. You're going to think I'm crazy, but that doll just talked to me."

Bill walked over to Marian and put his hand on her shoulder. Before he could say anything, Sabine jumped to her feet. She ran out of the room screaming.

"You thought I was crazy!"

She stomped upstairs and slammed her door so hard, things rattled within the house.

Marian sat and cried. She rocked herself back and forth.

"What is going on? What have I done?"

"Marian. Stop. Get a grip here. I need you to tell me what happened upstairs, then we have to talk with Sabine."

Bill pulled a handkerchief out of his pocket and handed it to Marian. She sniffled and wiped her tears.

"I went upstairs and apparently said something to myself. Anyway, that doll started questioning me. She got angrier and had an attitude about me being surprised at her talking. I ran out of the room."

"You're sure you heard the doll talking to you?"

"Yes, Bill. I'm sure. I figured you'd think I was stark raving mad and now Sabine thinks we see her as being crazy as well. We need to speak with her."

They tip toed up the stairs and stood outside Sabine's bedroom door for a minute. They could hear she was having a conversation. Bill looked at Marian, who shrugged her shoulders. Then Marian lightly tapped on Sabine's door.

They could hear Sabine saying, "I told you they would come up."

Then she called out louder, "The door is open."

Bill and Marian opened the door and saw Sabine sitting on her bed, with Samantha propped up against the pillows. They were facing each other. Sabine turned her head to look at her parents.

"So, you're here. What do you want to tell me?"

"Sabine, we came up to talk with you," said Marian.

"Sure you did, after realizing you insinuated I was crazy. Just like you."

Bill said, "No Sabine..."

Before he could say anymore, Sabine started yelling. Marian tried to say something. Bill raised his voice. No one could hear what anyone was saying; everyone kept getting louder and louder. No one heard the house phone ringing. One would think 'all hell broke loose' that evening in Sabine's bedroom.

Sabine glanced toward the bed. She saw Samantha going to jump from the bed. Sabine shrieked.

Bill and Marian froze.

Sabine grabbed her and placed her back on the bed. Samantha said, "Finally. All of you are quiet. You make me sick. Even though you all have one another, you can't be happy. You're constantly at each other's throats. I thought I'd get another chance with a family; instead, it looks like I'm stuck here."

Sabine reached out to grab Samantha, but Samantha backed away.

"Really? Do you think I want you hugging me right now?"

"But, but..."

Samantha continued, "Don't interrupt me. I know you are sad and hurt. I know your parents don't understand everything you are going through. But you have parents. You are all together. After finding myself locked up alone in the dark, I recognize being with those you love you is most important. Sabine, look at your parents. They love you. Don't be so hard on them. Help them understand what you are feeling so you can all work it out together. Your fighting makes me want to dive off the bed and hit the floor. We realize I'll break if I jump, but being broken will be better than living with all of you fighting."

Bill cleared his throat, took Marian's hand, and they walked over to Sabine.

Bill said, "You know, Sabine, for a doll, Samantha exhibits much wisdom. What do you say we stop fighting, sit down and talk about what is bothering you?"

Sabine looked from her dad to Samantha. Slowly, she shook her head in agreement, reached out to pick up Samantha.

"Yeah, let's sit and talk. I'm bringing Samantha with me."

The three hugged. If you looked closely, you'd see Samantha smiling.

December Is

only a memory
Remaking remembrances of days past
some sweet
some mundane
Holiday songs
gone from the public square
Trees once adorned with lights and baubles
now tossed by the curb
Crumpled wrapping paper fills the garbage bins

December marks the end of the calendar year
A new year has arrived
like an unblemished babe awaiting impact
of what the world lays on the babe
or the impact the babe has on others

So for us
the new year comes
It can be a clean slate
A time for new beginnings
or a holding place for the past's baggage

Baggage from the past
you can choose to toss
Gone is the looking backwards
and lingering regrets
With a clean slate
and heart full of gratitude
I have a new start

About the Author

From a young age, Linda developed and enjoyed an avid interest in the written word. Her love of reading grew into the dream to write. She has lived in numerous places within the United States and Europe. Travel provides an opportunity to experience varied cultures. Linda is a student of behavior and believes, life is the journey. Besides regional cultures, she's interested in understanding people and relationships; natural beauty; creativity and how God works in these various aspects of life.

Writing presents opportunities to bring these interests together.

Linda enjoys the camaraderie of writers both nearby and from afar. She finds inspiration, reward and constructive criticism of great value when interacting with other writers and is motivated by these experiences.

Her books display a variety in writing style, yet each addresses something important to her and of interest to the larger community. They are available on Amazon.

Blog: www.JourneyToTheHeights.com

Thank you for reading *Clouds, Dreams & Fantasy.* I hope you enjoyed it. If you did, please help other readers find this book:

1. The Kindle version of this book is lendable, so send it to a friend you think might like it so they can discover me, too. (Terms of lending established by "Lending for Kindle.")
2. Help other people find this book by writing a review on Amazon. Other than word of mouth, reviews are the primary way people find books. I appreciate you helping me in this way.
3. Check out my website: journeytotheheights.com
4. Sign up for new releases by using the "Sign Me Up" page on my website. You'll hear about the next book as soon as it is available.
5. Come 'follow' my Facebook page, Linda Flynn

www.ingramcontent.com/pod-product-compliance
Lightning Source LLC
Chambersburg PA
CBHW050924030726
47503CB00007BB/2459